Falling for Jun

DEDICATION

To all those who transformed from victim to survivor.

CONTENTS

ACKNOWLEDGEMENTS

The cover features a photo of K Street in Downtown Sacramento, and was taken by *Chasing Olives Photography*, a husband and wife partnership serving Sacramento and the surrounding area.

CHAPTER 1

He hated weddings.

Well, to be fair, that wasn't exactly an accurate assessment of what he thought about weddings. He enjoyed the atmosphere weddings created, and couldn't recall having ever been to one that he hadn't enjoyed.

Weddings always brought an incredible sense of anticipation and excitement for seeing the bride and groom at their best. There was a collective feeling of joy as family, friends, and strangers came together to celebrate two lives merging into one.

He entered the room and took in the vibrant colors of the flowers and decorations. People of all ages and sizes filled the church and took their seats, ready for love to take center stage, their faces aglow as they whispered greetings to each other.

Looking around reminded him that he appreciated the unique features of places of fellowship and worship. From modest churches with rows of chairs instead of pews and simple, unadorned walls to massive chapels with towering ceilings and large crosses. Each possessed a spiritual ambience that demanded quiet and reverence whether or not one was religious. This church was a combination of both under the purple and white flowers decked out at each end of the pews. A moderate sized cross was suspended above a simple white pulpit. Light seeped in from the windows, softening the mood with its glow.

He liked weddings, Jun decided as he took his seat with his family. What he hated was attending weddings with his mother.

His parents, who had both been born and raised in Japan, never hid the fact that their marriage had been arranged by their own parents, as was common in that day and age. In Ayaka Koboyashi's mind, there was no reason she shouldn't do the same for her own children.

The fact that they had immigrated to the United States in the late 1970s when his father accepted a position in software engineering—a place where arranged marriages were far from common—meant very little to Ayaka. For comfort and survival, they kept close ties to the Japanese community in San Francisco, and as a result, there was no shortage of potential candidates for him and his sister.

Weddings were the perfect setting for her to play matchmaker, whether he wanted to be matched or not. If he didn't keep an eye on her, or the potential women she could lasso, he would spend the reception speed dating.

This, at least, was growth on his mother's part. She let him be slightly involved in the process of choosing a woman for him even though his answer was almost always no.

Jun's gaze followed his parents, focusing on his mother, as they quickly left their seats to speak with another guest. He heard the rise and fall of their Japanese as they spoke to a distant relative or friend – he wasn't sure which. Relaxing a bit, he scanned the bride's side of the church, searching for potential women his mother might target.

That the groom was a cousin complicated things for him. Alex was two years younger than Jun's thirty. He could already hear his mother comparing him to her nephew, younger and married, while Jun remained unattached and growing older by the day.

Being single came with perks he just wasn't ready to part with. He traveled whenever, wherever, and as often as he wanted to. It didn't matter if he went with a group or by himself. He actually preferred traveling alone. It meant that he didn't have to consider the needs, wants, interests and desires of anyone but his own, and as a result, the entire experience was considerably less stressful than it was when he traveled with others.

He designed his home to his exact specifications, and used his free time as he chose. Really, the benefits of being single were endless.

And when he was ready to enjoy some female company, he dated. Or had dated until recently, he acknowledged with a frown. There was a surprising and unexpected sense of boredom that accompanied the prospect of going on a date despite the fact that Sacramento was full of beautiful Asian women.

Restlessness nipped at his heels as he tried and failed to get at the root of the problem. His only and most reliable solution was to go on vacation.

It was no accident that he planned his vacation to immediately follow the wedding. After several failed attempts to match him with some unsuspecting guest, Jun knew his mother would nag and lecture him for days. To avoid both, he would leave the country for two weeks. And assuage his guilt by bringing back several presents for her.

"You can relax," Mika said. "I doubt mom will be looking to set you up with anyone from the bride's side this time around."

Jun glanced down at his sister who sat cross-legged in the pew beside him, her shimmery blue dress pooling around her ankles. Her sleek, black hair was pulled back in a simple bun and left her face open to forecast the traits of her Japanese heritage. She had small, half moon eyes that casually took in the crowd before focusing on him. He returned his gaze to the sea of guests, considering this new information.

"What makes you so sure?"

Mika lifted carefully shaped eyebrows. "You don't remember, do you?"

"Remember what?"

"Oh, you'll see," she said with a smug smile.

Jun shrugged. He didn't make a habit of following his extended families every move. Keeping tabs on his sister and parents was hard enough with their busy schedules. He preferred to keep his circles small. But as he took closer notice of the bride's guests, he felt there was something about Alex and his future wife that he should remember, especially given Mika's cryptic response.

It was considerably more racially diverse than he was used to. Instead of an endless sea of Japanese faces, he saw several African American faces mixed in the crowd.

Then the music cued and guests moved to sit. Jun angled his body toward the center aisle as the wedding party entered. The obvious hit him when the maid of honor, dressed in a royal purple gown that complemented the rich chocolate tones of her skin, was escorted down the aisle.

How had he forgotten that the bride was African American?

Hadn't his mother talked about that for months when their engagement was announced? It was always a big deal when a member of the Japanese community married an outsider. It was a bigger deal that Alex's bride was African American. Or at least it was to his parents and their generation. While he was surprised, there was no denying that, for his generation at least, interracial dating was as common as dating within the race.

He wouldn't have to worry about his mother playing matchmaker after all. While part of him was annoyed by his parent's lack of open-mindedness, he couldn't deny that this was a fortunate turn of events. Ridiculously pleased, Jun stood as the bride's music cued, a grin playing on his handsome face.

Then simply stared in awe as she started down the aisle.

Stunning was too weak a word to describe her. Her long, heart shaped face radiated beauty. Her eyes were a clear and bright brown that focused with pure love and excitement on Alex as she walked toward him. The soft white of her strapless wedding gown tastefully highlighted her generous curves. Hair that was pixie short managed to be both feminine and flirty, and gave him a bit of insight to what he was sure was a bright and fun personality.

The attraction he felt was instant and surprising. He could handle an attraction to Alex's bride, compliment him on having the good sense to hold on to such a beauty. But what he couldn't handle, what he couldn't wrap around his head, was the jealousy that turned in his stomach and sent his mind racing.

He only dated Asian women. He enjoyed looking at women, found beautiful and attractive ones in all shapes, sizes, and colors. But he only dated Asian women. And yet, a part of him, the part that was bored and restless, stood at attention, and he found himself wanting a woman just like her for his own.

Jun watched the couple exchange vows and make promises of happily ever after and wanted, for the first time, what his cousin had with a fierceness that left him feeling hollow inside.

∞∞∞∞∞∞∞

"Maybe you should date an African American woman," Mika said suddenly.

Jun watched San Francisco fly by in a blur of colors from the passenger window and contemplated on how to respond to his sister when he had been reluctantly considering that very idea throughout the night.

The reception had been a lively celebration. The two cultures, joined in holy matrimony, danced and consumed alcohol together more seamlessly than he would have expected. But then again, alcohol was the great equalizer. Still, even as he saw that the blending could work, Jun convinced himself that what Alex had wasn't meant for him.

But his sister surprised him. As expected, his mother hadn't tried to pair him with anyone, he didn't think he had anything to worry about.

"You're my matchmaker now?"

Mika shrugged. "It's different. You like different because you usually do what's expected of you."

Now he was really interested. "Is that right? Explain that to me."

"You're a stereotype. Typical Japanese, typical Asian, really. Straight As. College. Medical school. Dentistry. Career. Date Asian women. One predictable move after the other. So you travel all the time to do something different. You'd bore yourself to death otherwise."

Jun frowned. "I'm not that bad."

"Okay, so that's too different for you. At least date a white chick."

"This is the strangest conversation I've ever had with you, and I'm the one who convinced you that you had imaginary friends."

Mika laughed, easing off the freeway and into San Francisco Airport traffic. "You didn't find any of those black women attractive?"

"Of course they're attractive."

"You just wouldn't date them. You are so Asian."

"Uh, thanks?"

"Get out of my car." Chuckling, she pulled to the curb. "Have a predictable amount of fun."

"I know envy when I hear it," he said as he climbed out and moved to the trunk to pull out his bags.

Mika rolled down the passenger window. "That's boredom, *niisan*. I'll be doing this same routine again in another six months when you get tired of your next round of Asian dating. But, at least I always get a nice gift out of it."

"Asian dating? You need new friends, Mika" he called out as he walked away.

He rolled his shoulders in an attempt to ease the tension he suddenly felt there. This trip was about relaxing. And yes, doing something different. He needed and craved it. He liked exploring new people and cultures. Traveling gave him that.

He didn't need to change his dating preferences to meet that need. This trip would chase the restlessness and boredom away. When he returned, he would ease right back into the dating scene and life would be back to the way it was supposed to be.

CHAPTER 2

A two-week vacation in Crete had been all that he hoped it would be, so it surprised him that he still woke up feeling restless. There had been hiking through the Samaria Gorge, with its towering mountains, lush greenery, and air so pure that he felt light headed.

He gave the Palace of Knossos two days of his time so he could attempt to capture its beauty and mystique with his camera. He sailed across waters full of color and life and lounged on beaches with sand as soft as silk.

When he arrived home, he went right to his room, collapsed on the bed, and slept for twelve hours straight. He woke, feeling refreshed, to unpack his bags and do laundry.

He checked in with his family and friends, reviewed his work schedule for the next two weeks, and closed the book on a vacation most could only dream of.

And yet, two weeks later, Jun found he was itching to escape the everyday monotony again.

Dangling long legs that made him five foot eight over the bed, he glanced around his room and pushed a hand through straight black hair that trailed down past his shoulders. The queen size bed sat on a simple wooden bed frame he had picked up at a second hand store in Berkeley, and was flanked by tall, narrow bedside tables in the same color.

The room itself was plain and boring, except for the walls. They held an assortment of picture frames with photos he had taken of all the places he had been. A quick glance usually helped ease some of the restlessness, but he wasn't having any success this morning.

Glancing at the clock, Jun pushed to his feet and dragged himself to the master bath. Thirty minutes later, he jogged downstairs, dressed and ready for work. He had a quick breakfast of scrambled eggs, turkey sausage, and lightly buttered wheat toast.

Gone were the days of eating whatever delightful dish he came across in Crete. He didn't worry about putting on weight, but he liked to stay active and healthy. He worked hard to maintain broad, muscular shoulders, defined arms, and a narrow waist in the kitchen as much as he did in his gym.

Dropping his dishes in the sink for later, he picked up his keys and headed for the garage. He was pulling out when he saw the four-door sedan maneuver into the third-car garage of his neighbor's house. As it had since last week, his interest piqued. The Halls had bought the house a year before, but he had never seen this little white car before.

Who was this new tenant who arrived at seven in the morning? It was an odd time to come home. It was another mystery he couldn't solve, at least not yet. He was a good friend of the Halls so it was only a matter of time before he found out. If only he could find the cause of his restlessness with the same amount of ease.

It took twenty minutes to reach downtown Sacramento. It was a maze of one-way streets, office buildings of mostly the same height, and enough skyscrapers to count on two hands.

It was home to Old Sacramento, a historical landmark, with western-style buildings from the late 1800s. On the other side of the American River, the Ziggurat building, known as the Pyramid due to its resemblance to Egyptian pyramids, waited for nightfall before it filled the skyline with light. The views from the commute from Natomas settled his nerves, even with traffic.

Despite the burst of the housing bubble that began to turn Natomas from miles and miles of empty fields to a healthy spread of shopping centers and homes, the community was filled to the max. Homes were sold and rented on a daily basis.

He had bought his own cookie cutter house two years ago for half of what it would have cost during the peak of the housing boom. The money he saved had been used to turn it into a green home that would rival those in Seattle.

Besides obtaining his PhD from the University of Washington, the city had also instilled a love for sustainable, green living, so his house was overflowing with modern green technology.

It took another ten minutes to navigate the busy downtown streets before he reached Pierce Family Dentistry. The life of a dentist wasn't exactly filled with excitement, but being a partner afforded him several luxuries. The Lexus hybrid he parked in an employee parking spot was one, but money and time ranked the top of his list.

Jun was paid well, and Sacramento's low cost of

living made it possible to take at least one two-week vacation every year. And its location was perfect for weekend trips to Napa Valley, San Francisco, Yosemite National Park, or Lake Tahoe. His mother would tell him the cause of his restlessness was too much time and money on his hands, and that settling down would fix him.

He didn't know a man alive who wanted to be fixed.

Jun stepped inside and into a cozy reception area that held a soft, gray loveseat and one matching couch. Three black side tables held books and magazines, and were frequently, and meticulously, reorganized by their receptionist. The wall of windows behind the loveseat let in just enough light to make the room feel cheery. A pot of fresh, colorful flowers finished off the room by perfuming the cool, air-conditioned air with its floral scent.

There was a patient fidgeting on the couch and another being checked in by Evelyn Jones. She was a short woman of only five feet, with hair that was rarely ever one color. This week, dark red hair with blond highlights stood out against her pale skin. She glanced up at him briefly before returning her focus to the patient, intent, he was sure, on seeing that the paperwork was properly filled out.

Evelyn buzzed him through and he moved down the hall to the office he shared with Dustin. Their desks were backed up against each other as they rarely worked in the same room at the same time. A coat hanger sat on the wall above their desks and held his lab coat. He tossed his keys and wallet inside the top drawer of his desk, then, settling down in the chair, he read over his patient's charts for the day.

Restlessness returned full force and he found himself struggling to focus. Usually he didn't feel this way until several months after a two-week vacation. A quick weekend trip to the Bay Area beat back the urge to escape for another month or two. Then the planning and excitement of an upcoming trip kept him satisfied until he was onboard the plane. Why was he desperate to escape when he had barely been back long enough to develop all of his photos from Crete?

"It's a little early for day dreaming."

Dustin Pierce breezed into the room, wearing a bright red dress shirt that stood out against his pale skin and white lab coat. He was just under six feet tall, with long facial features and bright green eyes that frowned down at him.

Jun merely grinned in return and leaned back in his chair. "Thinking about my date tonight."

Dustin snorted. "Would it be too much to hope that this is the same woman from last week?"

"Yeah. That wasn't going to work."

"I've heard that one before."

Jun merely shrugged and began stacking the charts. "You've got a great memory, mom."

"I just don't get why you would pass up a meal with Penelope for a woman you probably won't see again."

Jun frowned. "Why do you have to bring her into this?"

"She started walking last night," Dustin said with an excited smile that spoke of fatherly pride.

Jun's face lit up in excitement, his thoughts on the petite one year old with curly auburn hair. "That's great, D! I told you she'd get to it when she was ready. I can't wait to see her."

"So cancel your date tonight."

He laughed. "Maybe I can wait. I need the distraction from a woman who isn't in diapers. I'll come by over the weekend."

"Yeah, yeah. Get to work."

"After you, Dr. Pierce."

∞∞∞∞∞∞

Janet was the type of woman he usually dated. Her hair was jet black, her skin pale, her body slim and straight, and her ethnicity Asian. Japanese, Chinese, Korean, Vietnamese, or Hmong—it didn't matter much to him.

Her smile had been flirtatious throughout the evening, and the soft scent of her perfume had been inviting. He remembered commenting on it on their first date last month, and was flattered that she had thought to wear it again. She made it clear that she was interested in more than a few casual dates.

Janet worked at the Department of Education not far from his office. They had crossed paths one scorching summer day during one of his rare lunch trips outside the office.

He had been attracted to perky cheeks on a round, flat face. She had been chatting happily with a friend or coworker. When said friend or coworker left for a refill, he had taken that opportunity to ask permission to call her. His forwardness was usually rewarded, and that moment had been no exception.

It hadn't stopped him from completely blowing their date.

Jun paused for a moment to frown at his reflection

in his car window. Ducking down to the bucket of soapy water on the ground, he dipped his towel in the water so he could cover the window with suds.

Instead of waking with his hands on Janet, he was spending this warm, sunny Saturday morning washing his car. The day's restlessness had spilled over on to his date, making it difficult to focus on and participate in conversation.

If he was honest with himself, and he usually was, he hadn't been overly interested in her. Somewhere between their first and last date, his attraction to her had completely vanished. He hadn't felt anything that night.

But even that wasn't true, he admitted grudgingly. He had felt something, but his date hadn't been the cause.

The instant desire that had ignited in his belly had been caused by another woman at the restaurant. The skirt of her long, blue strapless dress had moved in time with hips that swayed effortlessly as she moved to her table. A thick, black belt brought his attention to a beautiful curvy figure. Hair that was black and curly danced around a face the color of coffee.

But it had been her smile that made his heart race. It was devastating in its beauty, blinding in its brightness, and rich with pure happiness. When she sat with her back to him, he felt as though she had stolen the very air he breathed.

Jun threw his towel in the bucket and picked up the hose. He wished he could wash the image of that woman away as easily as he did the soap on his car.

He would never see her again to start, and she was nothing like the women he usually went for. While he found women of every ethnicity attractive, he tended not to be attracted to the idea of pursuing something more than friendship. His instant, physical attraction to the African American beauty left him more than a little confused.

And oddly enough, he felt a little less restless.

His conversation with Mika before he left for Crete crept up from the recesses of his mind. It was just that he had been set in his ways for a few years now.

While he never went to the same place twice, everything about his life followed along the same predictable path. Go to work, visit family, visit friends, date a few women, and go on vacation. Repeat.

Maybe it was time for something different, like Mika suggested. His body was obviously ready and willing to experience something different. His brain just needed to catch up.

Liking the idea already, Jun retrieved a new towel from the garage and began drying his car. He would expand his dating pool instead of limiting himself to Asian women.

Instead of his usual weekend trips to the Bay Area, he could take a quick flight to Los Angeles, San Diego, or Las Vegas. That was good enough. Pleased, he snatched up the bucket and walked down to the end of the driveway.

He heard his neighbor's garage open and after glancing up, saw the tail end of the white sedan. Seconds later, the little vehicle was backing out of the garage. He would solve one more mystery today, it seemed.

Dumping out the water, he stood and offered up a wave and grin as the vehicle passed him.

And there, seated behind the wheel offering that same, devastating smile, was the woman who ruined his date last night.

"Uh…"

Not knowing what else to say, Jun walked up the driveway and decided he needed to pay his neighbors a visit before the weekend was done.

∞∞∞∞∞∞∞

Jun was a few blocks from home when Ruben and Nathan cruised up to him on their bikes. The jog around North Natomas Regional Park had been a much-needed distraction, but now he felt primed for whatever morsels of information his friend could give him.

Glancing over at Ruben Hall, Jun saw a steady and sophisticated African American man. He had dressed his lean figure casually in khaki shorts and a green t-shirt with a logo Jun didn't recognize.

At thirty-three, his ability to maintain a childlike wonder about the world meant he frequently found trouble for him and his son to get into. Ruben and Jun had bonded instantly over football. As the season was only a week away, he imagined they would be spending a lot of their time together over the next few months.

Like his younger brother Phillip, Nathan was a perfectly handsome blend of African and Mexican American. At seven, Nathan needed to know everything about everything, and sometimes, if he didn't get any answers, he saw a little of his mother Maya come out.

Maya was outspoken, blunt, and impossible not to

love. And when she resorted to speaking Spanish, she was impossibly scary.

Phillip was a rambunctious three year old who believed anyone who came into his world was another player in whatever game he happened to decide to play at that moment.

As a whole, the Halls were emotional, loud, chatty, flawed, and loved without judgment. That's what made them different from the average family.

Since they had moved in one year ago, he had been welcome into their home as a beloved family member. He wasn't expected or required to return the sentiment, but the Halls were irresistible. There had been as many dinners at their home as there had been in his.

He genuinely enjoyed spending time with them. And yet, he couldn't remember meeting or seeing the woman who now plagued his thoughts. The Halls had frequent family gatherings, but he was almost certain he had never met this woman.

"Hey Jun!" Nathan called as he brought his bright blue bike to a stop. He walked his feet on the sides of it to keep pace with Jun. "Did you like Crete? What was it like? Did you bring me anything?"

"Yes. Awesome. Why would I do that?" Jun answered, grinning over at the curly haired boy. "Hey Ruben."

Ruben walked his bike beside Nathan's. "Welcome back. We haven't seen you around since you got back."

"I've been avoiding the interrogation," he said, nodding his head in Nathan's direction.

Undeterred, Nathan eyed Jun determinedly. "Did you visit any monasteries? What were they like?"

When Jun slanted a look his way, a sheepish smile filled Ruben's oval shaped face. "I may have helped him with an Internet search or two."

"Oh yeah? Well I guess I'll just send those books back to Crete. Who needs them when you've got the Internet?"

Nathan's eyes lit up. "No, no! I'll take the books! Thanks Jun!"

They turned at the sound of a horn, and the little white sedan sped by. Jun felt his blood hum in surprised anticipation. A sinking feeling in his stomach immediately followed it when Nathan shouted excitedly.

"Aunty!" He hopped on his bike and sped off.

Jun stuck his hands in his pockets and nodded toward the house where Nathan dumped his bike to race up the driveway. "Aunty?"

"My sister, Valerie. She moved here from San Diego the weekend you left for Crete."

For a quick second he saw his neighbor's sister in a bikini under the San Diego sun. Guilt lodged in his throat. "Don't think I've met her."

"Probably not. She's been hoping to move back this way for a while now, so she kept her traveling to a minimum."

"I think you've mentioned her before. Between your family and Maya's family, I lose track of who is who."

Ruben chuckled. "Me too. Well, you'll get to know her better than the others. She'll be staying with us until she finds her own place. Hey Val."

Jun moved slowly up Ruben's driveway, grateful for the sunglasses he had thought to grab as he watched Valerie. She wore one of those dresses that stopped at her knees in the front, but flowed to her feet in the back. The style fascinated him. This one was the color of honey with two thick brown stripes at the hem and highlighted curves he had never truly paid attention to on other women.

Her hair was pulled back in a loose bun, so he saw the pure affection light up her eyes when she smiled down at Nathan. Her smile, and his attraction to her, was much more devastating up close.

"How come you're not that helpful?" She asked, watching Nathan carry in her last grocery bag.

"Because I'm the oldest, and everyone has to do what I say."

Her mouth twisted in a scowl as she turned back to her brother. "I don't know how anyone tolerates you."

Valerie replaced her scowl with an easy smile and turned toward Ruben's friend. He was watching them behind dark sunglasses, an amused smile settled on his full lips. Curious, she stepped forward, her hand held out.

"Hi. I'm Valerie."

Jun met her halfway, removing his glasses with one hand as he extended the other to take hers. Their eyes met, just as he wanted, and his smile grew when he saw the mild surprise in hers. He had an unexpected urge to brush his thumb over her wrist before he let go.

"Jun. Like the month, but minus the 'e'. I live next door. I've had to tolerate him for a year, and I started looking for a new place two months into it."

Valerie grinned now, pleased with his answer. "Need a roommate?"

"Suits me." Ruben said with a casual shrug. "No

refund on the rent though."

His thoughts took a nosedive at her innocent suggestion. "Ah, I'll let you know. So what was so special about Sacramento that you ditched sunny San Diego?"

Her smile faltered a bit. "What's better than ragging on your family?"

He noticed that her smile didn't quite reach her eyes, and he wondered why a simple question elicited such a reaction. "Um, San Diego?"

Valerie shrugged. "If you've seen one beach, you've seen them all."

Ruben laughed. "Ouch. That has to be a devastating answer to someone who travels like Jun does."

Jun feigned a blank look. "I'm still trying to process what she said."

Valerie worked to keep the smile from her face, enjoying his sense of humor, something that didn't go unnoticed by Jun.

"So you're a rolling stone?"

"I like to think I have more in common with Waldo."

Valerie laughed lightly, understanding the reference. "Where's Waldo been recently?"

"I just got back from Crete."

Valerie pursed her lips, more than a little impressed, and now even more curious about the man. "Greece's largest island. Must have been nice."

"Like going to Mission Beach," he said with a wide grin.

"Haha, how funny. I see why you two are BFFs."

Ruben gave her a light shove. "What boy doesn't enjoy tormenting his little sister?"

Valerie rolled her eyes. "Boy being the key word. I'm going in. It was nice meeting you."

"Likewise," he said, then with a smile, added, "See you around, Valerie."

"Finally. Now we can talk about something cool. Like football," Ruben suggested. "There's a game next Sunday."

CHAPTER 3

There had been promise in his voice, Valerie thought curiously as she placed groceries on shelves or in the refrigerator. She wouldn't have noticed it, wouldn't have suspected anything behind the casual phrase if not for the deliberate way he had introduced himself. He had removed his glasses in the same casual way gentlemen of the old days would tip their hat to a lady.

It should have struck her as polite, but when their eyes met, she knew he had meant for that moment to be personal and intimate. That friendly smile had lit up his face just enough to bring out his cheekbones and told her he was introducing himself not as her brother's neighbor, but as a man who was interested in a woman.

Valerie paused in front of the refrigerator, annoyed with the direction of her thoughts. Why was she immediately suspicious that the man had an ulterior motive after their first introduction? He had been nice, and had an easy sense of humor that had made her laugh and smile. There was just no reason to be suspicious.

Turning, she faced the kitchen and focused on the rest of the food she needed to put away. The light colored wooden cabinets framed the kitchen in a fat U shape that allowed several people to move around without rubbing elbows. The granite countertops picked up on that light brown color and were mixed attractively with black.

The counters were now littered with food, providing evidence that Nathan had emptied out many of the bags haphazardly, obviously looking for some deliciously unhealthy snack.

Valerie couldn't help but smile, and hated knowing he would have been disappointed. She knew that Maya kept the pantry free of snacks of the unhealthy variety as much as possible, allowing them only on holidays or when it was some special event.

So it was fruits, vegetables, and other whole foods that she placed in the refrigerator and pantry. Since it was her night to make dinner, she left out the ingredients she would need and took out others as she worked. When she was done, she switched gears to marinate the salmon.

"Hi, Aunty! Bye, Aunty!" Nathan called as he raced through the kitchen and out through the garage.

She heard Ruben and Jun's laughter before the door slammed behind her nephew. Feeling more positive now that she didn't have bitter thoughts of San Diego running through her head, Valerie allowed her thoughts to veer toward Jun again.

She had heard Nathan mention him before, but had assumed he had been speaking of a classmate. She would never have pictured the long, lean, and muscular man casually dressed in black basketball shorts and a red tank that she had met today.

He had a long, square face and thick eyebrows that drew attention to eyes the color of dark chocolate. He had a refreshingly witty personality and a handsome smile, which had become a tad bit exceptional when he grinned. His hair had been tied up. It made her wonder how long it was and what he might look like when it was down.

Which she had no business wondering, she told herself harshly. Wondering about things like that was why she ran into trouble in San Diego, she recalled, thinking of her ex. She squeezed lemon onto the salmon with more force than necessary as she brought Damien Winston's image to mind. He was a man whose looks were too devastating to be described with simple words like handsome and attractive.

At six foot two, Damien was a tall, dark glass of liquid sex, both in civilian clothes and in his Navy uniform. He used his charm and spectacular sex to court her, and then used it against her like a weapon until she realized, two years later, that she had been little more than his hostage.

When she told him she wanted to break up, Damien had flipped, displaying rage so ripe that it had scared her roommate enough to call the police. Admittedly, she had never seen him so angry, and what she had seen that day had terrified her.

She brushed off her roommate's initial suggestion to file a restraining order, but when the angry calls and text continued for two days straight, she thought twice. When he began attacking her on social media or messaging her through their mutual friend's accounts after she blocked him, she told herself she should reconsider.

When he showed up one afternoon at her job, she took the rest of the day off and went straight to the police station and picked up the forms.

When he came by her apartment again, she told him what was prepared to do if he didn't back off. The cold look in his eyes had chilled her to the bone, but he quietly agreed to give her space until she returned to her senses. It didn't shock her that he believed that she had wanted him back and she realized then that one day he might force her hand. She didn't want any part in ruining his military career, so she made a hard decision.

Over the next six months, she set about systematically removing any trace of her life in San Diego. She deleted every social media and email account she had and ditched the cell phone number she had used since middle school. She changed bank accounts, sold or gave away unimportant possessions, and got a P.O. box. With her resignation in, she applied for positions in Sacramento, and waited patiently for the school year to end.

Luckily, she had a few trusted friends who could find out through social media connections and other acquaintances when Damien was deployed. The moment she got the dates, she booked her flight and let her family know she was on her way back to Sacramento.

Those were the days, she thought grimly as she covered the salmon with foil and placed it in the refrigerator. Of course, she had left out most of the details about why she decided to move and didn't ever plan on sharing them with her family, or anyone else.

It was embarrassing enough that she had stayed in an emotionally abusive relationship as long as she did. Her family didn't need to know about her mistake. All that mattered was that she felt free when she moved one month ago.

Sacramento wasn't exactly a new place for her. She had been born here, and had been raised in Lincoln Village, or what most called, The Village. The nickname suited the neighborhood as it had reflected the old adage "it takes a village to raise a child." It was a place where she could get in trouble and be cared for both at home and at her friends place, and the same was true for everyone on her block.

Her family had moved frequently in search of neighborhoods with the best schools. She had lived in, played in, traveled to, or passed through nearly every neighborhood the city had to offer, but the Village inevitably pulled them back. It wasn't until high school that her family moved to, and seemed to settle down in the city of Elk Grove, which was located just outside of South Sacramento.

After high school, she all but flocked to Southern California and never looked back. She attended San Diego State University for four years, graduated with a B.A. in Liberal Arts and completed the teacher-credentialing program. At twenty-three, she began teaching third grade. She never imagined that San Diego would be her home, but that is where she had been.

Now she was back in Sacramento, and had to discover herself, and her hometown all over again. Sacramento and its surrounding cities had changed as much as she had in the last ten years.

It wasn't exactly comforting to discover that her new self was suspicious of attractive men. Or maybe she was suspicious of her attraction to attractive men. Either way, she would have to work on moving past that. Shaking her head, Valerie tucked the empty grocery bags away in the pantry as her brother's wife breezed into the kitchen.

Maya wore loose fitting pants with a vibrant black and white pattern of various animals. It was paired with a peach tank that showcased her pear shaped body. Black hair, cut in shaggy layers, danced around her diamond shaped face as she glanced around the room.

Maya placed a hand on her heart as she turned to Valerie. "Did I ever tell you how grateful I am that you moved in?"

Valerie laughed and closed the pantry door. "Only about a million times. I warned you that living with Ruben would be like having a child."

"He's not a child when it matters," she said suggestively, a wicked grin spreading across her beautiful caramel face.

"Gross."

Her grin only widened. "Never that."

"So where's Phillip?" she asked, desperately needing to change the subject, and moved to a cabinet to grab a glass.

"Phillip's asleep. Finally," she said with a sigh and sat on the stool at the counter. "Where are my other boys?"

"Outside talking to your neighbor."

"Ah, Jun. Another child. Except when it matters, I bet."

"Only you would consider that," Valerie said, rolling her eyes as she filled her glass with water.

Maya eyed Valerie as she sat next to her, speculation written clearly on her face. "You didn't find him attractive?"

Valerie's thoughts returned to her earlier assessment of the man next door. "Yes, he is attractive."

"I'm going to allow that non-answer because you're making dinner tonight."

Valerie decided she would avoid any conversations centered on Jun when Maya was involved from here on out. "Gee, thanks sis."

The door leading to the garage opened up and she heard Ruben, Nathan, and Jun shout their goodbyes as the garage door closed. Nathan passed through the kitchen, a large book all but plastered to his face, another in the crook of his arm, and disappeared upstairs.

"Do you hear that?" Maya whispered.

Valerie looked around. "Uh…"

Ruben merely shook his head, smiling and rolling his eyes.

"It's so quiet. So wonderfully quiet," Maya whispered again and shut her eyes. "I think I'll take a nap of all things. Thank you, Jun."

"You know he'll be done with both books by the end of the week," Ruben said as he leaned into Maya, then responded to his sister's confused expression. "Jun brought Nathan some books from Crete. He's been bringing something back for Nathan during his travels since they met."

"Wow. That is very nice of him," Valerie said.

"Those two are so much alike. They have to know everything about everything."

"Shh!" Maya demanded. "You two are ruining my nap."

Ruben chuckled and kissed her cheek. "Go lay down. Then on Sunday, Jun and I will watch the boys while you and Val go shopping or have a spa day or whatever."

Maya lifted one eyebrow. "Game here on Sunday?"

Ruben's smile turned sheepish. "Yeah."

"This week keeps on getting better and better." Maya kissed Ruben noisily and slid off the stool. "Val, tell me where you want to go. I'm going to finish my nap!"

Valerie sipped her water, making a small noise of agreement as she considered the strange feeling of disappointment that she wouldn't get to spend time with her increasingly interesting and attractive neighbor.

CHAPTER 4

"You're distracted."

"Hmm?" Jun looked over his shoulder briefly to find Dustin leaning against the doorframe, his forehead sporting several wrinkles as it often did when he was trying to piece together a puzzle.

Dustin pointed a finger at the sink. "You've been rubbing that soap over your hands for a full minute. I timed it."

Jun placed his hands under the faucet and the sensor tripped the water on, allowing him to rinse his hands. He gave a casual shrug.

"You would too after a cleaning like that."

"Bull. Shit. You rarely get distracted. Irritable, antsy, restless—I have an unfortunate amount of experiences with those emotions, so distracted Jun sticks out like a man wearing socks with sandals."

"Or like a white guy wearing neon green?" He probed, speaking of Dustin's bright shirt. Jun grabbed a paper towel and dried his hands.

"It's lime, actually. Distracted and deflecting. What gives?"

Jun leaned back against the counter. He had hoped to pick Dustin's brain on what had been going through his own at some point, but he hadn't pictured doing so between appointments in their sterilization room. The L-shaped room was a page out of an HGTV magazine with its bold white upper cabinets and mahogany lower cabinets.

Much of the sterilization equipment had been built into the cabinetry so that it blended in rather than stood out. The rest was meticulously organized on the crisp white countertops. The room would go from tranquil to busy beehive once the assistants came in to sterilize.

Factoring in the promise of interruption, and the simple fact that he had other appointments, this was neither the time, nor the place to get into the maze of thoughts in his head.

"I'll cop to the distraction, but I can't give you the details on why just yet. Still hammering them out myself."

Dustin's eyebrows rose in surprise. "That bad?"

"That complicated."

Jun left it at that and went to work. Distracted.

He did his best to stay tuned in to his patients. Usually he was able to avoid slipping into autopilot during cleaning procedures, but his mind kept wandering to his neighbors.

Which was stupid, he told himself, slipping further into autopilot. He was making something complicated that wasn't even a something yet. So he was attracted to Ruben's sister—big deal. That's all it was at this point. It wasn't a big deal that he had gone out of his way every morning that week to make sure he waved to her when they passed each other.

And where the hell was she coming from at seven in the morning? She probably worked at night. Maybe in a secret sex club where people paid her to don leather and punish them with chains and whips.

His punishment, however, would come from Ruben, who would likely remove his hands for thinking of putting them on Valerie.

Fuck, he did it again. He realized, as he stared into his patient's mouth, cleaning tools in his hands, that he had zoned out, mentally unaware of the work he had done even as his hands moved to complete a task they'd performed millions of times over. He hated the feeling on the rare occasion he had driven home on autopilot, and hated it even more when he had a patient in his chair.

But, the work was done and, after a final inspection, adequately so, even if he hadn't given what he deemed a much needed dose of emotional care and attention. He turned things over to his assistant and went to wash up before heading into his office.

Distracted may not be the appropriate term to describe the way his head randomly picked up and dropped trains of thoughts. He couldn't seem to maintain a single logical thought before it crashed and burned into something else, and it was past time he dealt with it.

Dustin found him sitting in his chair, feet propped up on the desk as he played a game on his phone. Dustin lifted an eyebrow, pulled off his lab coat and hung it on the hook above his desk.

"What are you still doing here?"

"Meeting up with Tony for a beer at Pizza Rock," Jun said with a casual shrug, his fingers still moving across the screen as he played. "The one on K Street. Do you want to join before you go home to the wife and kid?"

Dustin retrieved his keys and wallet from his desk drawer, considered. "It's Thursday. No date tonight?"

Jun locked his phone and dropped his feet to the floor to push up from the desk. "Nah, no date."

"Distracted, deflecting, and dateless. There's a little voice in my head screaming: Danger, danger, danger!"

Jun clapped him on the back and pushed him toward the door. "You should really see a doctor about that."

They walked through reception, noted that it had been cleaned and tidied courtesy of the ever efficient Evelyn. The lights were off, so soft sunlight that wasn't blocked from the surrounding buildings filtered in from the windows and cast shadows over the floor. They moved to the door easily, avoided tables and furniture, and disengaged the automatic locks to let themselves out.

The heat hit them like a wave, nearly pushing them back as they moved down the street. It was common for Sacramento to be hit with an Indian summer in late September, but it had begun earlier this year, making the air and the temperature spike. He could already feel himself beginning to sweat as they passed darkened businesses closed for the day.

Cars cruised down the street, their noise filling the air with sound. If he listened closely, he could hear the occasional, and rare, honk of a horn. Sacramento wasn't a busy, bustling city like San Francisco or New York, so the streets were pretty tame. Traffic, both car and foot, would likely only increase as the dinner hour drew nearer.

Tony Cheng was waiting for them outside. His sleeves were rolled up, his tie loosened and the first button on his shirt undone. He held his suit jacket over his shoulder with one finger while his other hand held his phone.

Jun had been friends with Tony since elementary school, and it was always a little bit weird to see him dressed to the nines.

"I see you got your power suit on. Who were your rubbing elbows with today?"

Tony slipped his phone in his pocket. "The people who sign my paycheck. How's it going, Dustin?"

"Can't complain. Been a while since I've seen you," he said, opening the door for his friends.

Tony stepped inside the restaurant and arrowed toward the bar where the lights were dimmed down and several televisions showed postgame highlights for the week's football games.

"They're asking us to push and push hard in getting our suites booked and rented before the basketball season starts," he responded, tossing his jacket counter before sitting.

Once settled in, they ordered their beers.

"Sucks. How's it going?" Dustin asked.

"It's going. So. We going to discuss your feelings like girls or what?"

"Sounds tempting," Jun considered, scratching his jaw. "But I think this time around, I'll settle for short and sweet. So a woman walks into a restaurant, punches me so hard in the chest that I can't breathe."

Tony's eyebrows shot up. "Can I just point out that this is the first time you've had that kind of reaction to a woman in what, five, six years?"

"No, you can't," Jun insisted, taking a sip of his beer.

"That hot, huh?" Dustin added, appreciation in his

voice.

"Yeah," he said, shaking his head. "That hot. Next day, I find out she moved in next door with her family while I was on vacation."

Dustin stopped his glass before he could take a swig and stared at Jun in surprise. "No shit? So why the hell did you say it was complicated?"

"She lives next door. With her family," he added with some emphasis.

"I'm confused."

Jun snorted. "Of course the married man is confused. The concept of a regularly accessible sexual partner is so normal that you can't see the possible chance of that going wrong."

"No, I'm confused that the concept of a relationship going wrong is your normal."

That stung a bit, and he didn't care for it, especially since it was basically true. "I'm just throwing out possibilities right now."

"I'm surprised you're even thinking about it," Tony said. "Normally you dive right in."

"This isn't a normal circumstance."

Dustin placed his glass down and turned so he faced Jun fully. "So you're into her that much?"

"Are you going to let me finish?"

Dustin deliberately picked up his glass and drank.

"Second complication. She's my neighbor's baby sister. I really like this neighbor, we hang out all the time."

Now that Dustin understood. "And if you hook up and it goes south, you're living next door to a man who is likely plotting your very painful death."

"Exactly what I'd do if it were Mika."

"Shit, I guess that is complicated. Have I met

these neighbors?" Tony set his drink down and tried to recall Jun's neighbors. "I remember Ruben and his boys. Didn't know you had Asian neighbors."

"I don't," Jun said into his glass.

"You don't?"

"No."

Jun watched them both struggle to wrap their heads around that for a full thirty seconds.

It clicked for Tony first. "So this really hot chick who took your breath away – fuck you for making me say that corny shit out loud – is not Asian."

Jun took another drink. "Nope."

"Wow."

They drank in silence, each considering the situation with the full knowledge that this was new territory for them all. Dating your neighbor, who happened to be a good friend's sister was boggy ground on it's own. But interracial dating?

How could he give Jun advice on navigating that tricky arena? Dustin knew that while Jun had never discriminated against different types of Asian women, he had never fully explored interracial dating. Maybe Jun wasn't as comfortable with the idea as he wanted to be, which had to be revealing for Jun.

It was one thing to talk about being on the side of interracial dating, but it was another thing to practice what you preach. Which only left one question.

What was her ethnicity?

"I've only ever heard you talk about Ruben. So this woman, she's his sister?"

Jun finished his drink and pushed the glass toward the bartender. "Yeah."

"Huh."

"At first it sounded like a really good idea. Dating

an African American woman," he clarified.

Dustin rubbed a hand over his face. "Were you as shocked as I'm feeling right now?"

"No, not even a little. I started asking myself, is that the only kind of woman I'm interested in? And why is that? Is it because that's what my parents, especially my mother, expect of me? Or is it really what I want? After I got over the initial disappointment that I let a beautiful stranger ruin my date, I knew I had to figure it out. I've been bored with the dating scene, and maybe it was because I was only dating Asian women. And the only way to find out was to go out, meet a nice black woman and see where it went, all thanks to that beautiful stranger."

Dustin watched Jun dig his wallet out of his pocket when the bartender slid the bill in their direction. "So the idea was okay when it was some other woman, but not the woman who changed your outlook."

Jun placed his card in the folder. "Yeah, I guess there's that."

Dustin could tell his friend that he had that same reaction, those same thoughts, and the same look on his face when he decided to ask out the woman who changed the way he thought about everything, and the woman who would one day become his wife, but some realizations a man just had to come to on his own.

Tony finally spoke up. "You got a problem with interracial relationships?"

Jun added a tip, signed the receipt. "No. No," he repeated firmly. "But I feel like I'm looking for all kind of excuses for why it isn't a good idea for me."

"Maybe it isn't." Tony held up his hands when

Jun looked at him sharply. "I'm just saying. Don't get into something you're not one hundred percent okay with, especially with your friend's sister."

Jun stashed his card and wallet back in his pocket and pushed away from the bar. "I guess you've got all the answers."

"Free beer makes me smarter," Tony said, following Jun out.

Dustin laughed. "Same. Look, I'd say just get to know your new neighbor, and keep it as simple as that for now."

∞∞∞∞∞∞∞

Valerie was certain that she had just completed the week from hell.

It was her belief that her class of eighteen third graders went above and beyond their obligatory hazing of a new teacher at their school. While it was true that some of what she saw was pure and simple excitement from beginning a new school year in a new grade, Valerie hadn't been as prepared as she would have liked to be.

She supposed that was to be expected as she had been hired two weeks after the other teachers had returned from summer vacation. She had done the best she could to get her classroom ready in between training and orientations.

She realized that there was a big possibility that she would have to spend some of her weekend in the classroom making adjustments to the layout now that she knew her students a little better.

There were students picking fights and unfriendly cliques forming, while some students simply distracted their peers for the sake of it. She had already identified a small handful of students she would have to work really hard to build a relationship with. She could only assume that the next few weeks would get worse before they got better.

She had left school later than planned, and by the time she got on the road, Friday night traffic was in full effect. Her commute had taken forty-five minutes instead of the usual twenty. But instead of heading straight home, she pulled into a parking lot to face the most painful kind of traffic: after work grocery store traffic.

She had promised Nathan that she would make spaghetti, and he would never forgive her if she didn't keep her promise. Unfortunately, they didn't have any ingredients in the house.

So with aching feet and exhaustion threatening to drop her where she stood, Valerie pulled out her favorite perfume and gave herself a little spritz. Feeling a little energized with the scent surrounding her, she snagged a basket from the shopping cart return on her way inside and squared her shoulders to brave what came next.

She moved quickly through the produce department and snagged an onion, bell pepper, garlic, and mushrooms in record time. She sped through the pasta aisle, doing little more than a grab and toss of her favorite sauce and noodles.

She took her time in the meat department, careful to read the dates and prices on the ground beef before she headed to the bakery for garlic bread. Then she made her way to the registers with a little sigh.

Even with five registers open, there were no short

lines, so she took this moment of forced relaxation and appreciate that she had been able to gather all of her ingredients in only fifteen minutes. She estimated it would be another ten minutes before she got back to her car, and another five before she was home.

As long as she reminded herself that the weekend was only fifteen minutes away, she could do this.

Not that her weekend was packed with anything even remotely exciting. She would make a trip to the gym early tomorrow morning, and likely take a much-needed nap before heading to her classroom for the remainder of the afternoon.

She did have a few friends that still lived in Sacramento, but they wouldn't be going out for a night out on the town this weekend. The idea of it sounded completely cliché, but after her week, it would have been a nice reprieve. Some of the people she knew were just beginning to start a family and didn't have as much free time as she did. Or they were used to her being far away that they forgot she moved back.

But she would have Football Sunday. With Jun. She spent her morning commute to work with him on her mind, a feat, she was sure, he would have been pleased with since it was obviously his goal.

Every morning she went to the gym to take a six am group exercise class, and every morning she returned, he was there, just pulling out of his garage in time to wave goodbye with a handsome smile plastered on his face. He timed it that way, she was sure of it.

So she thought of him, trying to figure out what angle he would play to charm her into a date. She should be flattered, she told herself, but she just couldn't stand false chivalry. She would rather he just come out and say what he wanted rather than pretend to be something he wasn't in order to impress her.

And she was assuming again, she realized. Ever since she had ended things with Damien, Valerie had begun to assume that every chivalrous act, every charming smile that came from men was disingenuous.

It wasn't fair, but even after a year, she couldn't seem to let it go. It shouldn't have surprised her. In the moments where she forced herself to face the painful truth, she had known Damien for what he was a year into the relationship. She hadn't wanted to be alone. She needed the attention, the affection, even if it was given only to manipulate.

It had been hard to walk away, to accept that she had allowed herself to be used and manipulated. She wasn't ready to put herself out there only to risk repeating the same mistakes.

She paid for her groceries and placed the two bags back in the cart. Sighing, she pushed it outside, intending to return it to the cart section in the front of the store. She was just about to reach inside to retrieve her bags when a pair of pale, masculine hands snatched them up.

"Let me get that for you. You're parked over here, right?"

Jun pointed in the direction of where she parked and stopped short of turning when Valerie released an exasperated sigh. He looked at her, confused, when he saw the tense set of her jaw. She moved past him stiffly and pulled her keys out of her purse.

"Um, Valerie?"

She spun around, trying to contain the annoyance

and anger she knew she shouldn't feel toward someone who was just trying to help.

"What?"

Baffled by her frustrated response, he closed the gap between them and removed his sunglasses to get a good look at her. She wore a dark pair of skinny jeans and a black collared shirt with floral print.

Her hair was pulled back in a ponytail at the base of her neck and so her face was open for him to see clearly. Her brown eyes flashed annoyance and her lips were drawn tight in impatience. His eyes narrowed and tilted slightly in speculation.

"Are you annoyed with me because I'm helping you with your groceries?"

Now it was her turn to narrow her eyes. "Is that what you were doing? I thought you were walking off with my bags and I was just supposed to follow after you, no questions asked."

He felt the blush creeping up his neck, embarrassed to find that she was absolutely right. To give himself a moment, he turned to place the bags back in the cart.

"If you don't want me to help, you can say no."

Valerie sighed again. "It's a bit too late for that."

"No, it's not. I should have asked first. Valerie, may I help you take your bags to your car?"

"Why?"

"We're neighbors. I want to get to know you."

She shook her head and her keys and turned to walk toward her car. "Don't know what you hope to find out in the minute it takes to get to my car."

Jun slipped his sunglasses down over his eyes and grabbed the bags again, thinking he had learned so much about her already, and followed after her.

"I learned you know how to put a man in his place when he deserves it."

Valerie wrinkled her nose a bit, feeling remorseful. "Look, I—"

"Have nothing to apologize for. I earned it. But now I'm learning you may not have a mean bone in your body after all. Are you sugar, spice, and everything nice?"

"There's some chemical X mixed in there."

"Chemical what?"

Valerie shook her head, amused at herself for referencing Power Puff Girls. "Nothing. I spend too much time with kids, obviously."

"So, is this what's for dinner tonight?" He asked, fishing for an invite.

She was too distracted by how increasingly aware she was of his presence to notice. "My famous spaghetti. Here I am."

Jun heard the click of her trunk and lifted it up. It was empty but for the bucket of reusable bags in the corner, bags she hadn't taken in to the grocery store.

"You forgot something in there."

"Hmm?" She stepped closer to him and saw the bags she had forgotten to take inside. "Oh, yeah. I was in a rush."

"Okay, so now I know you're forgetful when you're in a rush. And you smell absolutely amazing."

An awkward silence settled between them as he placed the bags inside the trunk. When he stood, he realized she was staring at him as if he had grown a second head.

"What? I…"

He trailed off, realizing what he had done. What he had said. Valerie watched in morbid fascination as his face fell and a blush crept up from his neck until it covered his entire face. She didn't think she had ever made a man blush before, and was slightly baffled that she felt more than a little proud that she had done so.

"I said that out loud," he said in stunned disbelief.

She nodded and cleared her throat. "Ah, yes. Yes you did."

"I…Okay. Hmm. I'll see you around."

Valerie watched as he forcefully shoved his hands in the pockets of his faded blue jeans and walked back to the store. He wasn't as charming as he seemed, or wanted to be. It was actually kind of cute. Smiling at the idea, she closed her trunk and slid into the car.

CHAPTER 5

Jun carried the embarrassment with him all weekend, reliving that moment at Valerie's trunk whenever he failed to keep himself busy. Usually he was smooth and relaxed with women, but something about Valerie put him out of sorts.

He tried taking Dustin's advice, as it was the sanest idea he had right now, and keep it simple with her. And yet, the simple act of taking her groceries to her car had turned into the most complicated interaction with a woman to date.

He shook his head as he placed beer in a reusable bag, and then added some steaks and vegetable kabobs he had put together earlier that morning. Those one-on-one interactions would have to be limited until he got a better handle on her personality.

For now, keeping it simple might just mean hanging out with her where both of them were most comfortable – with her family.

He swung the bag over his shoulder, swept his keys off the counter and walked to the front door. Kicking off his house shoes, he stepped into his sandals and let himself out. He locked his door behind him, walked the short distance to his neighbors, and let himself in, knowing Ruben would be expecting him.

The warmth of their home surrounded him like a hearty welcoming hug, just as it always did. He felt his body relax, and prepared to enjoy the vivacious family. He called out, toeing off his shoes as he walked toward the kitchen.

He passed the family room where a chocolate colored couch sat against white walls. The floor was littered with cars and blocks, evidence that the boys had been at play. Two bold red accent chairs faced the windows and the entry, daring him to take a seat and enjoy the lush cushions.

The walls above the couch and on the entryway were covered with family photos both candid and posed. The spread always reminded him of the galleries he often visited on his cross-country trips, except the walls were far more cluttered. The bright happy faces drew him in as easily as those galleries did.

He paused now, scanning over them, to look for Valerie's image. How many times had he passed this wall, never noticing the woman who now plagued his thoughts? Countless times, he surmised, when he found a candid shot of her and Nathan when he had been younger.

They sat facing each other, hands inches away from their faces. Nathan's eyes were big and round, his mouth open in an oval to convey surprise. Valerie's eyes were filled with amusement and joy, her cheeks big and rounded from the smile that captured her entire face.

He found a few others in the mix and he realized that this was the first time he truly saw them. It was amazing what a change of perspective could do.

Jun continued past the family room. Behind those lush red chairs were a large table and six chairs, designating the space as the formal dining room. A half wall rose up to separate the formal dining room from the living room. This room held a small sectional in the same color as the couch in the family room. A large television framed the wall in front of it and was already set to the sports channel.

He realized that the house was entirely too quiet. He set his bag on the kitchen counter.

"Hey, anybody home?"

"Commercial break potty time," Ruben called from the bathroom.

There was a flush and the unmistakable sound of a toilet seat being closed before water splashed the sink. Jun began unpacking his bag just as the men emerged from the bathroom.

Jun raised his eyebrow in speculation as he took in the trio. "I've been in that bathroom. It's not big enough for the three of you."

Ruben chuckled and clapped Jun on the back. "Size, like privacy, is an illusion in the world of parenthood."

Phillip waved at him and dashed back to his toys while Nathan hung back to stand by the counter.

"Hi Jun!" Nathan called. "We read that Zeus was born in Crete. In a cave. Did you go there?"

Jun opened the fridge and moved some items around to make space for his beer and steaks. "Dikteon Cave. I spent a few hours there."

"That's so cool. Dad helped me find some stuff on the Internet, but we're going to go to the library on Tuesday."

"Oh yeah? I bet that's going to be great. Books are

better than the Internet."

Always delighted by the boy's enthusiasm for knowledge, Jun gave him a genuine smile as he set the six-pack next to a small container of spaghetti. He snagged two beers as his eyes narrowed, the wheels in his head turning. Was it wrong of him to pump the kid for info?

"Hey, you guys had spaghetti this weekend? Where was my invite?"

"Aunty made it on Friday. She makes the best spaghetti," he added.

"Oh yeah? Maybe I'll eat the rest of this here."

"No way! That's mine!"

Nathan dashed for the fridge just as Jun closed it. He threw himself against the door as Nathan attempted to open it.

"Sharing is caring, right? How about we ask your Aunty who can have it when she comes out of her room?"

Ruben snagged Nathan into a headlock and led him toward the family room. "She and Maya went out to do whatever it is that women do together."

"Well then I guess we'll do whatever it is that men do together," Jun said as he dug in a drawer for a bottle opener. After popping the tops on the beers, he went to the living room and collapsed on the sectional. Not sure if he was relieved or disappointed that Valerie was gone, he added, "I saw Valerie at the grocery store on Friday. First time a woman wanted to deck me for helping out with the grocery bags."

"You're kidding?" Ruben asked, surprise in his voice. He sat next to Jun and gratefully accepted the beer. "Glad to hear she's getting some back bone. Sorry she tested it out on you."

"You and me both." Curious now, he couldn't stop himself from pressing for more information. "I think I smoothed it over afterwards, but she didn't come home upset did she?"

"No, not that I remember. She was fine." Ruben took another pull from his beer and brought the night back, but now that he was thinking about her ex, it was all he could think about. "She used to date some controlling as—I mean control freak—for two years," he corrected, remembering he had kids around. "She's still bouncing back. You know, gaining confidence."

It was hard for him to picture a woman as beautiful as Valerie lacking in confidence. And harder for him to accept the low burning anger in his gut.

"I hope you decked him."

Ruben shook his head. "Only in my dreams. He's in San Diego. Just have to be satisfied that she dumped him and moved here."

The game switched on then, so all non-football related conversation ceased completely. But it didn't stop his thoughts from jumping back to Valerie. Two years with a controlling man? He imagined that her ex must have had a stellar public personality for Valerie to tolerate that kind of thing from a man.

He would have been incredibly charming, and Valerie incredibly naive. The image he conjured didn't vibe with the vibrant, sexy woman he already had in his head, but love, if that is what it had been, didn't always make sense. But the relationship had burned her badly enough for her to relocate five hundred miles away.

At least he understood why she snapped at him for taking her groceries.

He would have to be careful not to be too

charming, and definitely not come across as controlling. He would have to find a way to romance her on her terms, but in his way.

Which made about as much sense as his sudden decision to pursue her. He had been interested from the start, but he hadn't committed to the idea of pursuing her until just now. But he had to face facts.

She consumed much of his thoughts since that moment in the restaurant. And since seeing her again, that restlessness he had felt was all but gone. He only ever felt that way right before a vacation and the weeks after he returned.

Maybe all he needed to do was open up his dating pool to include more women of color. He had traveled the world, seen and appreciated women of all ethnicities, but he had only dated Asian women.

He still wasn't even sure why that was. He had been approached by white women before, but it never went anywhere beyond flirting.

Did he find Asian women more approachable than other women? Was he stuck in a cycle started in college? He guessed it was true that it was easier to date women who were familiar with his cultural background.

That other, unfamiliar world was limited to being visited and explored two times a year. He always considered himself open to change and to trying something different, but he had yet to meet a woman who sparked as much interest in him as Valerie had to make him change his dating habits.

It was time he made a change, he thought, and returned his attention the game.

The game had just ended when Valerie and Maya returned. The boys had passed out on the floor in the family room shortly after halftime. Ruben and Jun were sprawled on the living room couch, enjoying the lazy Sunday.

He eyed her over his bottle, careful not to show his open assessment, and appreciated the miles of gorgeous leg before they were interrupted by white shorts and a red and gray striped halter.

Maya breezed in and leaned over the back of the couch to kiss her husband. "I haven't shopped that much in months. Maybe years. I'm starving."

Ruben pushed himself from the couch. "Thought you might say that, so I put some things on the grill not ten minutes ago."

"That's why I married you. You wore my boys out?"

"They wore themselves out. You want some food too, Val?" Ruben asked as he headed for the backyard.

"Sure. Hi Jun."

Determined to keep it casual, Jun lifted his beer in greeting. "Hi."

Maya walked into the living room, scooped Phillip off the floor, and turned to go upstairs. "I'm going to change this guy. He reeks like a man."

"You're welcome!" Jun called, realizing that he and Valerie were alone. He climbed off the couch and made his way into the kitchen. He felt a sudden need to keep himself busy. "Want some wine? Ruben had it breathing for you two."

Valerie lifted her eyebrow and took a seat at one of the barstools at the kitchen counter. "No reason to say no to that."

Valerie watched him move around the kitchen in blue basketball shorts and a tattered gray t-shirt that read "U Dub." She couldn't recall finding a man in lounge wear so attractive before, but something about Jun got her juices going.

How could she be so attracted to a man she barely knew? His dark hair was tied up in a messy ponytail at his neck, and she felt her curiosity peak again. She didn't know many men who wore their hair long, and she was dying to see how long his was. Dying to get her hands on it.

"Thank you," she said when he placed a glass in front of her, clearing her throat a little. She sipped gingerly, watching with growing curiosity as he pulled plates and forks out like a man who lived here. "You seem to be right at home."

Ruben came in then, carrying a pan with delicious smelling meats. "Jun can often be found hanging around here whenever he isn't traveling, at Tony's or Dustin's, or visiting family. In that order."

"That's an interesting order."

"A necessary evil," Jun said with a grin. "It invariably turns into an inquisition when I go to my parents since they are impatient for me to settle down."

"Your rolling stone is showing," Valerie pointed out.

Jun covered his face. "Shit. Don't look!"

She laughed. "Your family is close by?"

"Close enough. They all live in the Bay Area," he said, catching movement from the family room. "I like coming to Ruben's to see my next victim, I mean, patient."

Nathan walked into the kitchen, rubbing the sleep from his eyes. "Hey!"

Jun grinned. "It's only a matter of time before I'm

called to pull out all of Nathan's teeth."

Nathan hid behind Valerie. "Well, my Aunty will give you detention!"

Jun widened his eyes dramatically and took a huge step backward. "Detention?"

"Yeah!" Nathan shouted, feeling more confident. "Teachers can do that."

Jun narrowed his eyes and looked between Valerie and Nathan. "Is this true? Are you the dreaded Teacher?"

Valerie couldn't stop her smile. "I teach third grade."

Jun nodded gravely. "You win this round, tiny human."

Maya sauntered down the stairs, Phillip following close behind her. "Nathan, go wash up. You probably smell like a man too."

Nathan groaned, but obeyed.

Jun began fixing himself a plate. "I'm probably dating myself, but I don't remember third grade detention."

Valerie struggled to keep the smile off her face and affected a very serious expression. "Then you were a good student."

"You're very scary, Ms. Hall. How long did it take you to master that look?"

Now she did grin. "Oh, about a year into it."

"And you've been using it for how many years?"

"Seven."

Jun took his plate to the eat-in kitchen space where another table sat. This space doubled as the kid's art area, so there were floor shelves that held tools of the trade. The table was smaller than the dining room table, but still sat six comfortably. It was a plain, light colored and sturdy wood that could hold up to the abuse of two children. He took a seat next to Nathan, who sat patiently for his plate.

"Yeah. Scary."

Valerie sat across from Nathan. "Not scarier than the dentist."

"True, true. But that comes with the package. Teachers? Not necessarily."

Soon they were all settled at the table, sharing stories of past teachers, both of the scary and non-scary variety. The playful banter kept the mood light and casual. It was the simple atmosphere he wanted that would help him figure out just how to approach her.

But he felt his attention being pulled back to her more than he felt was appropriate when her brother was sitting next to her. He wasn't sure if he should be relieved or annoyed that nothing in her manner indicated that she might be aware of the extra attention he was failing not to give to her.

But while Ruben and Valerie remained oblivious, Maya's sharp eyes caught nearly every subtle glance Jun made in Valerie's direction. Those were the eyes of a man assessing his prey. It was exactly the kind of attention she thought Val needed. But Val, beautiful, unaware of her own sexual prowess Val, did nothing more than spare him a handful of curious looks. Well, big sis would fix that.

"No, no. Val and I will take care of it," Maya insisted after dinner, pushing Jun out the kitchen. "Thanks for cooking. Boys, tell Jun goodnight."

With goodnights and goodbyes taken care of, Ruben escorted the boys upstairs.

"Val, walk Jun to the door while I get things

started."

Valerie stopped dead, a dish she had been about to stack frozen in her hand. "What?"

Maya turned her back to Jun and smiled sweetly at Valerie. "Walk him out and lock up. Thanks, darling."

"Sure…" Valerie stacked the dish next to the sink. She gave Maya a small smile, knowing exactly what the woman was up to.

"Goodnight, Maya," Jun said with a wave, a bright smile on his face.

"'Night, Jun."

Valerie led him to the door. "I can't help but feel silly doing this. You're more like a family member than a guest."

"There's a game next week. We'll watch it at my place, and I can walk you out," he promised as he slipped on his sandals.

"I'm not a football fan."

"That's not a good enough reason to miss out on food and conversation," he said, pausing in the doorway. "I hope my utterly embarrassing high school faux pas didn't put you off."

Valerie paused with her hand on the door and gave a slight tilt of her head, her confusion evident. "Faux pas?"

"Hmm. I'm not sure which is worse. The fact that I told you that you smelled amazing, or that you don't remember it happening."

"Oh, hah!" She gave a sly smile. "Hard to forget something that red. Oh! There it is again!"

He struggled to stop the blush from getting out of control. "Glad to see my embarrassment amuses you."

She grinned. "Exactly. You didn't put me off at

all."

"That's really, really good," he said quietly, leaning toward her and moving his hand around her to open the door slightly. "Because I have to say it again. You smell incredible. It's a little bit distracting."

Valerie pressed herself back against the wall and stared up at him, words caught up in the butterflies dancing in her stomach.

"If you change your mind about football, I'd love to have you." Because he was watching her closely, he saw the slight hitch in her breath his words elicited. "Would you mind letting Ruben know?"

"Sure. No problem. Can do."

He smiled at her before pulling the door open. Stepping out, he turned and said, "I'll see you around, Ms. Hall."

Valerie shut the door and locked it, grateful for the sticky hot air that seemed to jump-start her brain again. She walked back to the kitchen and as soon as she entered, Maya turned, her eyes inspecting, as she looked at her.

"I half expected you to come back rumpled," she said, turning back to the sink.

Valerie went back to the kitchen table, hoping her voice didn't give her away. "What? Why?"

"That man had his eyes on you all night, no doubt thinking about having his hands on you all night."

"That's ridiculous," she said in denial, even as she continued to reel from the blatant pass he made at her. "You've had stars in your eyes since I broke up with Damien."

Maya began rinsing dishes. "Sweetie, those were daggers, not stars. I've only tried to set you up with one, maybe two guys. This is different. I don't have to set this up. You just need to see what's in front of your face."

"And I should jump into a man's arms just because he's interested?" Valerie set more dishes on the counter next to the sink. She pulled a towel from a drawer, dipped it in the water and wrung it out.

"Don't treat him like Damien. That's not fair to either of you. It's been over a year, Valerie. It's time you open yourself up again and leave that mess behind you."

"I'm not interested."

"Is it because he's Asian? Japanese, I believe."

Valerie paused in wiping down the kitchen table. "Don't be ridiculous. His ethnicity has nothing to do with it."

"Then why?" Maya demanded, pushing the dishes into the sink water with a little more force than necessary.

"I'm not interested."

"He's got a fantastic body."

"Maya!" Valerie half choked, half laughed.

"And such intense eyes. If I noticed, you noticed."

"I'm not blind, just not interested in anything serious." Valerie stood next to Maya at the sink and began rinsing dishes before placing them on the drying rack.

"A date or two or even a few rolls between the sheets isn't serious."

"Oh. My. God. I can't believe I'm having this conversation with my brother's wife."

"Conversations like this are why I am your brother's wife. When he asks you out—"

"When?" She managed to choke out, unable to deny the inevitable when it was spoken out loud by someone else.

"When he asks you out, say yes. Take back control of your love life, Valerie. You've been without it for too long."

CHAPTER 6

"TGIF!" Valerie let out an excited squeal as "I Gotta Feeling" by The Black Eyed Peas came on the radio. Though it was an oldie, she turned the music louder, bouncing to the rhythm and grinning as she sang along. It was finally Friday, and tonight would definitely be a good night.

She had a really good week at school. On Monday, she started her students off by taking them through the process of creating rules and consequences. They had taken to the task eagerly and proudly, and worked hard to hold each other accountable throughout the week.

She expected the novelty would last at least two months, but she would enjoy it while it did. The new classroom configuration had also been a hit.

She ended up splitting the class into two L shaped groups, angling them slightly for a clear line of sight, and assigned seats in a boy-girl pattern. It eliminated the cliques from forming—for now—and prevented most distractions. The rest of the week had progressed with few bumps and bruises.

And at lunch today, Valerie had confirmed girl's night out with Gianna and London.

She had met Gianna and London in high school,

and had kept in touch, mostly via social media, since she had gone off to college. They had only been able to get together for dinner a few times since she moved back to Sacramento, but it had been as fun and crazy as it had been when they'd been younger.

Tonight, they were taking her downtown to show her the city had grown up as well.

In celebration of her wonderful week and to commemorate the weekend, she had gone shopping for the perfect girl's night out attire. It had been far too long since she had enjoyed a carefree night.

In the honeymoon stage of her relationship, Valerie had allowed herself to believe that Damien's jealousy was simply a sign of his desire to want her all to himself before he went out to sea for a few weeks or months.

Then came the emails, with their subtle digs and accusations of being unfaithful. And if his ship was underway, she had to go out of her way to find a quiet space to answer his calls, no matter where she was, or he had assumed she was out partying with another man.

Going out had caused more stress than joy as she invariably worried that she would have to deal with Damien's jealousy.

Valerie rolled her eyes in annoyance, mostly at herself, as she turned into her brother's neighborhood. She sat up and rolled her shoulders, shaking off the feeling and her thoughts of Damien. It was time to stop dwelling on every aspect of the past – including her own stupidity – and truly move forward. Tonight was a great time to start.

Because she made a quick stop at the shoe store near her house, she came from the opposite direction she usually did, and passed Jun's house first.

His single car garage was open, and she caught a glimpse of gym equipment that piqued her interest. She pulled into her garage, biting her lip as she considered.

Moving forward also meant accepting the fact that she had more than a few stray thoughts about Jun during the week.

Her thoughts had often spiraled back to that moment at the door where the slightly red faced Jun had given her butterflies. And with Maya in her head, urging her to take a chance, it would be a blatant lie to say she wasn't considering doing just that.

Maybe moving forward would have to start right now instead of tonight.

Decision made, she popped her trunk for later and checked the urge to primp. She pushed her door open and was immediately greeted with the 80s rock that blasted from Jun's garage. Slipping her keys in the pocket of her slacks, she made her way to his house.

As she approached the garage, she saw an adjustable bench and an impressive variety of hand weights stacked on a shelf against the wall. A power cage with a bar and pulley system stood gleaming behind it and was already racked with heavy plates.

Nodding her head in appreciation, Valerie moved into the garage and was even more impressed when she felt the give of the rubber that covered the garage floor.

She was admiring the dip and pull up handles on the power cage when Jun stepped into the garage. He eased the door closed, wanting a moment to watch her before she saw him.

She tucked a peach colored quarter sleeve blouse into wide legged navy slacks decorated with white polka dots. He couldn't help thinking that she looked like a quintessential teacher dressed like that.

Though none of his teachers had ever made him think about anything other than academics. With Valerie, his thoughts often veered to her soft scent, or her quick, beautiful smile.

Then there was the rolling laughter and the miles of leg he had been able to bask in at dinner on Sunday. He had never moved this slowly with a woman that interested him before and it was both irritating and intriguing. Necessary. He had to remind himself that it was necessary if he didn't want to scare her off.

He often wondered where she came from every morning. She always looked so calm and aware when she came home.

What was the sexy Ms. Hall up to before sunrise? It couldn't be drugs or alcohol. He recalled his earlier thoughts before they were introduced. Maybe her experience with her controlling ex-boyfriend had actually led her to BDSM, and she spent her nights practicing being a dominant.

Damn if the thought of her wearing leather and holding a whip didn't make him hard.

Taking a sip of the water he had gone inside to refill, he moved to the stereo to turn the music down, reminding himself that this was not the time for X-rated thoughts.

She turned quickly, a sheepish smile spreading across her face when she looked at him. He was wearing his hair in a tightly wrapped bun again and for some inexplicable reason it made her want to pout.

And again, though he was dressed casually in a grey sleeveless shirt and black basketball pants, he was no less attractive.

For one moment, she felt something akin to the struggle she imagined men felt when they forced themselves to make eye contact when all she really wanted to do was check out the byproduct of all this gym equipment.

Embarrassed by her thoughts, she began wandering again.

"Very, very nice setup you have here."

"Are you blushing, Ms. Hall?" He asked, grinning as he watched her turn the plates to read the weights.

Valerie pursed her lips to stop her smile. "What can I say? Gym equipment really does it for me. What do you bench press?"

He lifted an eyebrow at the question. "One eighty. You?"

"Seventy five. We do close to one hundred reps in the class I take so you have to keep it a little light to hit them all."

"No need to explain, that's an impressive weight." He couldn't help letting his gaze travel over her body. "I didn't know you worked out."

She was too busy looking at the hand weights to notice his open assessment. "Yeah. I go to the gym over on Del Paso."

It clicked then. "Is that where you sneak off to every morning?"

She turned to face him, amused by the wonder in his voice. "I wouldn't call it sneaking. What did you think I was doing?"

The pretty image of her in leather formed in his

head again. And with a better idea of just what her body looked like, the image was a lot clearer than it had been. Feeling the stirrings of a semi hard-on, he walked to the bar to adjust the weights, and his shorts.

"Are you blushing?"

He turned back when she started laughing. "You really want to know what I thought?"

Her laughter died down as he approached her, a heated expression on his face. Warning bells alarmed and she forgot why she had come over in the first place.

"I should get going."

He placed a hand on her arm to stop her. "It's a really interesting story. How about I tell you over dinner tonight?"

His hand slid down her arm and captured her hand. He tugged her back, his thumb stroking her wrist. Her scent drifted up to him again, washed over him and filled him with need.

He wanted to press his lips to the curve of her neck and just breathe there. Valerie sucked in a breath and stepped back. He moved forward.

"I would tell you now, but I'm not sure I would be able to stop myself from turning fantasy into reality."

The look in his eyes shot heat straight to her core. She had an idea that whatever he had been thinking, it ultimately ended with the two of them naked. And now she was thinking about it too.

"I have plans."

The tiny spark of jealousy cleared his head enough to make him remember his own plans for tonight. "Oh, yeah. So do I."

"Excuse me?" She tried to pull her hand away

again.

Jun laughed. "I'm sorry, I didn't mean it like that, but that got your pulse racing."

She pulled her hand away and stepped back. And though he really didn't want to, he let her go.

"That's a bit fast, don't you think?"

Jun gave a weak smile. "I was actually just thinking about how slow I was moving."

Considering, she clasped her hands behind her back. Hadn't she come over here to take a step forward? To leave the past behind her and embrace whatever the future held? So why wasn't she taking what he offered?

"I'm going out with some friends tonight. Dinner and some place called Dive Bar."

Jun desperately wished for pockets so could keep his hands busy. He really wanted his hands on her.

"I know it. My friends and I usually drop by there when we're downtown."

"Well," she said, taking a deep breath to find her courage. "Maybe you should drop by there around ten tonight."

It took everything he had not to react in any way to that small, small step. "Maybe I will."

Valerie smiled then and turned away, finding her confidence. "You will."

Jun rocked on his heels as he watched her walk away. "Yeah. I will."

∞∞∞∞∞∞∞

She didn't tell London and Gianna that she invited him out, not wanting to shift the focus of their night to men.

Instead, she set it aside, and took a ride share to a place called Punch Bowl Social. It, and the new Golden 1 Center just steps away, hadn't existed when she left Sacramento all those years ago.

The arena had opened up in 2016 and was home to their NBA team, the Sacramento Kings. The new arena had taken over the space that was once known as Downtown Plaza and had replaced it with the bustling and thriving area now known as Downtown Commons.

They ate at Punch Bowl while singing karaoke. When they were finished, they got more drinks and flirted as they moved from arcade to table games.

It was 10:30 when they finally made it to Dive Bar. It was a dark and crowded little bar on K Street, and her heart beat in time with the music.

She was grateful when London and Gianna left her alone at the bar. She needed a moment to compose herself before she saw him. When she did, she nearly swallowed her tongue.

He wore his hair down.

It shocked her to the core, seeing his long, rectangular face framed by straight black locks that fell just past his shoulders. His eyes, brown and focused like an animal on the hunt, stood out against his face and brightened when they met hers across the crowded bar.

She stood there, the bottle of beer halfway to her lips, as he came closer. Desire, hot and sticky, worked its way from the bottom of her stomach and up to the center of her chest when a sly smile spread across his lips.

Valerie sipped her beer, and then turned to set it on the bar behind her. When she turned back, he was standing there, dressed in a white collared shirt and a dark pair of jeans. She had to tilt her head back to see his face, and caught the scent of his cologne as she did.

In some distant part of her mind she heard warning bells, but was too focused on him to bring them to the forefront. Part of her was sure she would regret it later. Another part didn't care.

"Hi."

"Hi."

Jun shifted closer, leaned in, and watched her eyes widen a bit. He was making her nervous. "It's crowded tonight. Have the mermaids come out yet?"

Valerie looked up at the massive aquarium above the bar where salt-water fish swam idly by and people dressed as merpeople made appearances.

"A bit ago, but the bartender said they come out every half hour on weekends, so we should see them again soon."

"Lucky us. I'm going to get a beer. Can I get you something?"

"Sure. Whatever beer you're having is fine."

Valerie switched places with him, feeling awkward after their dull conversation, and let her eyes search for her friends as he ordered. She needed a buffer between her and this overwhelming attraction that was humming inside her. He had been eye candy before, and a source of curious interest, but now she was afraid she had just opened herself up to the same pattern she had with Damien.

"London got distracted," Gianna shouted over the music, her brown eyes sparkling with mischief as she slithered up to Valerie's side.

Valerie immediately knew that to be a lie. Decked

in a short, white spaghetti strap dress with a red floral pattern, Gianna Maffucci would likely draw the attention of many a man with her olive colored skin and curvaceous body. Her brunette hair danced in wild curls around her long, expressive face and her quick, infectious smile could easily charm anyone.

"She stopped and talked to like five guys," she said, rolling her eyes dramatically.

"And somehow they all have your number," London said dryly, standing right behind Gianna.

At nearly six feet, London Henderson stood a full head taller than Gianna and always reminded Valerie of runway models. She certainly had the body for one. She had wrapped her slim figure in a tight sky blue strapless dress that popped against her dark chocolate skin. Her short, tapered fade showed off the impressive bone structure in her face and bright smile – though she wasn't smiling at the moment.

"Weird, right?" Gianna grinned. "Well, let's squeeze in here and get another drink!"

Jun turned then, holding a beer in each hand. He saw her friends and paused in the act of handing the beer to Valerie. "Wow. I think you'll have a much easier time getting a drink than I did. Is my tongue hanging out of my mouth?"

"No, you're good. Ah, thanks," Valerie said, accepting the beer and then gesturing to him with it. "Gianna, London – this is Jun. Jun – Gianna and London."

"Hello, ladies. Would it be weird if I said wow again? Wow. You want this one too? I can probably get another in half the time if the bartender sees I'm buying for three gorgeous women."

Gianna accepted the beer, her interest piqued.

"Why, thank you."

"Really, Jun, you don't have to," Valerie objected.

"I interrupted your ladies night to say hi – it's the least I could do."

"What a gentlemen," Gianna said, snatching the beer from Valerie and all but shoving her closer to Jun. "Help him out, Val. Flash that beautiful smile of yours and get one for yourselves."

They walked away. Despite the crowed, Valerie felt like they were completely alone.

Jun turned sideways so she slid in front of him. The side of her body brushed against the center of his chest as she faced the bar. He looked down a bit to take in the green sequined dress that highlighted her coke bottle figure. It was an image he understood and thought he appreciated when he had seen other women with that shape.

But up close and personal, he was sure he would spend the rest of the night wondering just how her body would fit against his. He saw now that her hair was dreaded, and the small locs curled sweetly around her face.

She had done something fancy to her eyes with makeup and was wearing that scent she had on the other day. He leaned in a little so he wouldn't have to shout over the blaring music.

"So if Gianna's the subtle one, I can't imagine what London is like."

Shaking her head, Valerie gave him a small smile. "I'm sorry."

"Why? I came here for the express purpose of hitting on you. I just wasn't expecting the hot wingman."

"Are you always so brazen?" She asked, grateful

that the bartender was finally ready to take her order.

Jun got out his wallet and paid for the drinks. When he had his wallet secured away, he leaned in again so only she could hear him. "Probably. Except with you, I've been having embarrassing trunk moments."

Valerie looked up at him and the ends of his hair tickled her face. "At least you're not turning red this time."

"And you are. At least on the inside."

"That obvious?"

"Takes a nervous wreck to know one."

She smirked, handing him his drink. "Now you're mocking me."

"I've only ever dated Asian women, and while I know you're not an alien, I feel like I'm treating you like one. Fuck, I don't even know why I said that. Shut the fuck up, Jun." He leaned back and took a deep pull from his drink, not surprised when she started laughing at him.

"I don't even know what to say to that."

"Can't say that I blame you." He looked up and nodded his head toward the mermaid that slipped into the water. "Ah, here she is. A nice, safe subject to talk about now that I've made another not so amazing impression on you. Where do you think she gets the tail?"

Valerie shook her head in amusement. "A little shop down on 36th street."

"Ah. I think I know the one. I'm pretty sure I've driven past it on my way to work. Mermaids N' Things, right?"

Valerie chuckled, unconsciously leaning in closer to hear him. "I think that's the one. So your office is downtown?"

"A few blocks from here, actually. Not actually near our made up mermaid store. I just come straight down J on the way in."

"Have you ever stopped by to watch the mermaids after work?"

A couple eased in behind him, trying to gain access to the bar. Without thinking, he set his hand on her hip and moved her along with him as he stepped away from the bar. He saw something flitter over her face before he dropped his hand and cleared his throat, feeling unsure of his moves again.

"I haven't. We usually go to the pizza place next door."

"Why have you only dated Asian women?" Valerie blurted out, surprising both of them. She blamed the trail of heat that arrowed straight between her legs when he had touched her. It clouded her rational thoughts.

"Damn. I was hoping you'd forget I said that."

His obvious discomfort made her smile and relax a bit. "Why? Do you think I'd find something like that upsetting?"

"Yes? No? I don't know, honestly. It never seemed like a bad thing until a month ago. Now I feel like I've insulted women everywhere."

Curiosity made her relax further. "I imagine you're not the only person on the planet who only dates people who look like them. Culture can be a comforting thing."

"It can also trap you, and close you off to the rest of the world."

"Yes, there's that too. But you like to travel. Everywhere from what Nathan has told me. So you haven't closed yourself off completely."

"Have you dated men outside your ethnicity?"

"A few dates here and there in college, but nothing that lasted beyond a month. I think my crush history covers all ethnicities."

"Damn. I'm awful."

Valerie laughed. "You're not. It's just how some people are."

"Well, I'm changing."

"Why?"

"I saw you," he said simply, his eyes meeting hers.

"Ah," was all she could say as she looked away. She took another pull of her beer as he watched her.

"You absolutely ruined a date I was on," he said accusingly, trying to lighten the mood.

Shocked eyes flew back to his. "I what?"

"I saw you," he repeated, looking up at the tank, and forced himself to keep his tone light, even comical. "On my second date with Janet. We were at BJs in Natomas. I don't usually take dates that close to home, or there of all places, but, to be fair to you and unfair to Janet, I was already losing interest. So there I was, sitting across from this stunning Asian woman, and you walk by with that bright smile of yours. Close to that one," he said, looking down in time to see her smile and point to it with his bottle.

Valerie bit her lip to stop it from spreading further.

Jun grinned in return, pleased that his confession amused her instead of turning her off. "Naturally the rest of the date was a disaster because I was distracted by you. I kept hearing you and who I assume must have been Gianna and London laughing. I couldn't concentrate. Then of course, as punishment from the universe for disappointing Janet and taking a date to

Natomas, I learned you're my neighbor."

Valerie cleared her throat. Downed her beer. Cleared her throat again. "Not what I was expecting you to say."

"So far nothing about this is what I was expecting. I'm not used to being interested in a woman who somehow always ends up with the ball in her court, even as I try to steal it away."

"I'm not….that's not…I don't."

Jun stepped closer, placed his hands gently on her hips and pulled her in until their bodies were pressed together. The warmth of him spread through her body, setting her nerves ablaze and her heart racing.

His hair curtained her face so she felt consumed by him. The scent of him overwhelmed her as he leaned toward her, his lips all but brushing her ear as he spoke. For one fleeting moment she wished he would press his lips against her neck or nibble on her ear. She had to keep her hands trapped at her sides in fear that she might do something rash.

Like spear her hands in all that luscious hair and drag his mouth to hers.

"I wanted to seduce you tonight."

You have, she wanted to say, but the words stuck in her throat.

"But I'm going to make a mess of this thing growing between us by telling you again how amazing you smell. How beautiful you look tonight. I'm going to think about how it would have felt if I'd given in to the need to taste your lips for the rest of the night. You sparked a change in me, so I'm going to put the ball in your court again, Valerie. For some reason, that is more important to me than seducing you."

One of his hands left her hip and slipped over her

hand, prying away the empty bottle she gripped like a lifeline. When he moved away to place them on the bar, she felt the absence of his presence like she was just coming up for air after being underwater a minute longer than was safe. She had to resist the urge to draw in a deep breath and breathe through her nose instead.

"I should find my friends," he sighed reluctantly. "And let you get back to yours."

Valerie risked looking up at him and watched his heated glance travel one last time over her body. "Yeah, sure."

Jun turned, searching the crowd until he saw Gianna and London hugging the wall on the far side of the bar, chatting and stealing an occasional glance their way. Valerie jumped when he placed his hand on the small of her back. He angled his body to make a path to her friends as he moved forward.

"Ladies, thanks for letting me steal Val for a bit."

Gianna merely lifted her drink. "It was a fair trade."

"Not even close," he said. "It was nice meeting you. See you around, Valerie."

"Yeah."

All three women watched him walk away in silence.

"Wait!" Gianna exclaimed, finally breaking the silence. "Unless he's got some crazy memory, I did not see numbers exchanged."

London rolled her eyes. "Maybe he already has it. They obviously know each other."

"Oooh, backstory. Spill," Gianna demanded, holding her beer up to Valerie like a microphone.

Valerie snatched it and gulped it down, earning

surprised looks from her friends. "He doesn't have my number, and he doesn't need it. He's my neighbor. I met him like two weeks ago."

She filled them in on the rest. For some reason it both calmed and alarmed her since it gave her a very clear picture of where this was heading. She didn't feel as ready to move forward as she had earlier in the day.

"Well, I might need to move to Natomas," Gianna said, fanning herself dramatically. "Find me a man who can generate as much heat as the two of you were."

"Oh, god," she said, thoroughly embarrassed.

London, more sympathetic than their friend, put a gentle arm around Valerie's shoulder. "Balls in your court. What are you going to do with that kind of power?"

"Power? What power? I feel like he's turned me inside out."

Gianna clucked her tongue. "Sweetie, sweetie," she said, sighing. "You have that man in the palm of your hand, and you didn't even have to do anything to get him there."

"You have the power to decide when—I won't say if because let's face it, you're into him - this thing goes any further between you," London clarified. "You won't have to wait and wonder why he hasn't asked you out yet—but he will. How long are you going to keep him waiting?"

She hadn't thought of it that way, and now that she was, she couldn't help but worry he wouldn't have to wait too long.

CHAPTER 7

"Well, good morning," Maya greeted Valerie with surprise. "No gym for you today? Must have been a crazy girls night out."

"Oh yeah," she said sarcastically, making her way to the coffee maker. "We were girls gone wild. I decided to follow my crazy night with a lazy Saturday morning."

Maya wiggled her eyebrows. "Pour me a cup of coffee and dish!"

Valerie retrieved two mugs from the cabinet above and set them down. "I didn't get home until one am."

"What? All the way until one am? You wild thing!"

"Blame the mermaids. Who knew watching people swim with fish could be so fascinating?"

Maya gratefully accepted the mug, sipped gingerly. "I've heard of this magical, child free place. Did you do any fishing?"

Valerie leaned against the counter to face Maya. As she had been prepared for such a question, her response was casual.

"Unfortunately, no. Though it wasn't from a lack of trying."

"Next time I insist that you have a one night stand." Valerie choked on her coffee, much to Maya's amusement. "Mind helping me with breakfast?"

"Will it get you to stop talking about my sex life?"

Maya considered as she moved toward the fridge to pull out the fixings. "Sure, why not?"

Fortunately for Valerie, Maya was true to her word. Conversation stayed pleasantly on safe topics before things turned chaotic when the boys, her brother included, came downstairs, whining for breakfast.

Wanting to keep the chaos down to a minimum, Valerie ordered them to set the table, deciding that they would serve breakfast family style. While the scent of bacon and sausage filled the air, she pulled plates, bowls, and serving ware from cabinets. Maya let Ruben and Nathan finish with the scrambled eggs while she tackled the last of the pancakes.

Valerie handed a plate of bacon to Phillip, then walked behind him while he slowly and carefully made his way to the table. Moments later, they were all seated at the table, passing plates, bowls, and syrup until their plates were filled.

Maya sipped a bit of water. "We should have invited Jun."

"Yeah!" Nathan shouted. "He hasn't come over for breakfast in a while."

"I'm sure that will change," she said, a suspicious smile spreading across her face. "After all, he is very interested in dating your Aunty."

Both Ruben and Valerie choked on their food.

"What's dating?"

"It's when two people who like each other go out and do something special together," she said casually, handing Ruben his glass of orange juice.

Valerie glared over at Maya with watering eyes.

"Maya, you're insane."

She shrugged, unoffended. "While he has absolutely no say in who you date, your brother needs to be prepared for the inevitable as I'm sure he is too dense to have seen what's been in front of his face since you two met."

"I…don't know what to say…"

"You don't need to say anything, sweetie. What they do is none of your business."

"Or yours," Valerie said, without heat, knowing that Maya's meddling was meant to help them avoid drama. She had been too caught up in what she was feeling to recognize that something happening between her and Jun could and would impact his relationship with Ruben.

All wide-eyed innocence, Maya responded, "Oh, of course it's not."

"When are you going to dating, Aunty?" Nathan asked innocently.

"Going on a date," Maya corrected, earning a glare from Ruben and Valerie.

"When are you going on a date?"

"We aren't. Do you want some more pancakes?"

"Why not? Don't you like Jun?"

"Hey, Nathan, do you think we should go to the park today?" Ruben asked, desperate to change the subject.

"Yes! Can we invite Jun? He can go on a date with us."

Both Valerie and Ruben groaned in response, and Maya burst out laughing.

∞∞∞∞∞∞∞∞

Valerie spent the remainder of her weekend keeping busy with household chores, lesson plans, and a side of heavy adulting by updating her budget.

She sat on her plush green bedspread, feet curled up under her, as she looked over her spreadsheet. Morning sunlight filtered in through the window, brightening the light gray walls. She had set the radio on low, more interested in background noise than anything else after she had finished cleaning the first floor of the house.

The move from San Diego hadn't cost nearly as much as she had originally budgeted for. When she had made the decision to leave Damien and eventually San Diego, she had been overwhelmed with a desire for a fresh start.

She had donated nearly half of her closet and a few small pieces of furniture, leaving the larger pieces she had purchased in the apartment she had shared with her roommate, Claudia. Since most of her favorite films and TV shows were available through video streaming apps, she also sold most of her DVD collection.

Ruben and Maya had made a surprise visit just a week before she planned to move, and had insisted on taking two suitcases of whatever she had been willing to pack up.

With fewer items to ship, she had more space to pack in her car when she finally made the drive to Sacramento. Additionally, what she saved in renting, splitting utility bills, and other expenses meant she could shift money for a much larger student loan payment.

At this rate, she should be able to pay off her student loan earlier than planned. Biting her lip, she checked her budget again and committed to paying it off in December instead of March.

That change ultimately brought her closer to her home buying goal. She had a good portion of a down payment saved up, and her parents had offered to give her $5,000. She hadn't yet started to search for homes, but thought it might be a good idea to get connected to a realtor soon.

Valerie opened up her email to find the list of realtors that Maya had sent before she moved and found a new message from her former roommate in San Diego. The smile that began forming on her lips vanished when she saw the first word in the sentence.

To: Mallorie Smith

From: Claudia Newman

Subject: Check out this news article

Dickhead came by a few weeks ago. NBD—we both figured he'd drop by when he got back to flex his muscles as if the very sight of them would have you begging for forgiveness. The dick.

But there was a break in at Turtleback last night and I just about freaked when I heard the news this morning.

Who the hell breaks into an elementary school? What could they possibly steal that's worth anything? They didn't say if anything was stolen but it just seemed way too coincidental to me that your old job gets broken into a few weeks after your ex comes around trying to find you. Just thought you should know.

In other news, I'm worried about Vivian. She and her boyfriend broke up recently after she found out he'd been cheating on her.

But instead of drowning her sorrows in ice cream and cheesy romantic comedies, she's gone full sex kitten! She's gone out every weekend since the break up and has hooked up with some rando. She seemed like such a great choice when we interviewed her to take over your lease, but I'm starting to think she fooled us both!

Anyway. Hope you're doing well!

- C

Holy fuck, she thought, slamming the laptop shut after she closed her email.

Valerie sprang up from the bed, her heart racing as she stared at the computer as if he would magically spring from it.

She felt herself fly back to that day, felt the sting of pain, the shock. Heart racing, she took several breaths, trying to calm her racing heart.

The seed of fear that she thought she had burned to ash sprouted instead, its sharp roots pricking her throat as she fought for calm.

No, she reminded herself. She wasn't going to feel this way. She left San Diego in fear, but she wasn't going to live with it. She refused to believe that there was a connection between the break in and her ex.

And even if he had broken into the school, she had been careful. The last address her old job had on file was the P.O. box in San Diego, and she had closed that before she left for Sacramento.

Since she enrolled in paperless billing for anything

important, the P.O. box didn't have a forwarding address either. There were only a very small handful of people who had her current contact information, and an even smaller number who knew she relocated to Sacramento.

She didn't even use her real name on her new email account. He would never be able to find out where she was.

And she refused to believe that he would risk ruining his career over their break up. The restraining order alone would have been damaging. Breaking and entering would surely get him kicked out. Damien loved being in the Navy more than anything else. He wouldn't do something like this.

Thinking it through helped her settle. She took a quick shower to smooth the edges and then donned a loose plaid romper the color of the sky.

Calmer now, she searched the house for her family, though she was fairly certain they were with the person she had been avoiding thinking about all weekend.

But now she needed the distraction, so she walked to Jun's house and rang the doorbell. The moment she heard the bell she began second-guessing herself. The man made her feel too many things, just like Damien had, and even though her friends said she had the power in this still unfolding dynamic, she wasn't exactly sure how to wield it.

Biting her lip, she debated going back home, nervous about being in Jun's space, about being around Jun, or any man at the moment.

But the door swung open, and she was greeted by Jun. He held a little girl in his arms and offered her a genuine grin when he saw her. Surprise lit her face, and she realized it had more to do with the feeling that washed over her when his eyes brightened after they met hers.

The remaining traces of panic and fear were wiped away and replaced with the same sense of safety and freedom she had felt when she first came back home. How did such a simple and welcoming gesture make her feel so calm?

"Ms. Hall! Glad you could make it. Come on in. It's half time so we're in the kitchen."

She took a deep breath and stepped into a room with a bold, black accent wall where several white-framed photos hung. The entryway closet was opened up and converted to fit a built in bench, with slots for shoes beneath it, though none of the guests had bothered to use it.

Stepping over the discarded shoes, she slipped out of her sandals and slowly followed after Jun. She looked at the sea of frames, which held what she could only assume were photos of his travels.

Beaches, temples, jungles, pyramids—here was the world and all its wonder framed on his wall. She had never known anyone who had traveled this much.

The family room held a long, dark blue L-shaped couch with gray throw pillows and a coffee table in a dark, almost burgundy wood that matched the entertainment center. Mounted above it was a flat screen TV so large that she wasn't sure what size it was.

On the other side of the couch, propped against the half wall separating the family and living room, was a long, narrow cabinet. The layout essentially mirrored her brother's home, but the feel here was all tasteful bachelor.

There was just a love seat and one chair that faced the fireplace and open windows in the living room. It surprised her how intimate that area felt.

The kitchen, with its bold black granite countertops sprinkled with flecks of white, held white cabinetry and top of the line stainless steel appliances. He hadn't held back here, she thought, and wondered just how much time and money he had spent renovating this home.

An attractive Asian man sat in one of the barstools wearing a Kings jersey. This confused her, since they had gathered to watch football. And the intense look he sent her also confused her.

It wasn't until Ruben stepped into the kitchen from the dining room that the man snapped out of whatever daze he had been in.

"Couldn't resist the lure of BBQ?"

"The carnivore in me finally took over." She glanced around, hoping for the comfort of female company. "Where's Maya?"

"Store run with Alena. I think she wanted a break from the testosterone."

"Well, the testosterone levels in this place could turn even a runway model into a tom boy."

"Val, this my friend, Tony. This is Ruben's sister, Valerie."

He wiggled his elbows in greeting since his hands were covered in food and he struggled to make eye contact with her. "Uh, nice to meet you."

Had she offended him? "Same. Sorry about the testosterone comment."

Tony smiled lightly. "Don't be. Now I'm thinking about runway models playing football."

"In lingerie?" Jun asked, the image making him

grin.

"Can you not talk about lingerie while holding my daughter, please?" Dustin snatched Penelope away before extending his hand out to Valerie. "I'm Dustin. My daughter, Penelope. My wife, Alena, is with Maya."

"I'm Valerie. It's nice to meet you, Dustin."

"What's lingerie?" Nathan asked from the dining room where he sat eating with Phillip.

"Gods gift to man. Would you like a drink, Valerie? Wine, beer?"

"Red?"

"Got it."

Jun went to a cabinet in the living room and retrieved a bottle of wine from the wine fridge. Pouring her a glass in the kitchen, he asked. "How are the children treating you?"

"Like the wicked witch of the west."

Jun laughed, then handed her the glass. "Send them my way. A few teeth pulled and they'll behave better than those two."

Valerie took a few sips before grabbing a plate. He watched her fill it with food, liking how she looked in his kitchen.

"Monkeys behave better than these two, but I wouldn't change a thing about them."

"Smell better too."

"I used your cologne, remember!" Nathan shouted, making all the adults laugh.

"Well said, kid."

Valerie sat with Dustin and the boys at the table to finish eating. Jun swept in and took Penelope again, who giggled when he tossed her up in the air. When Maya and Alena eventually returned, he was hunkered down on the floor, claiming a space before everyone moved to sit on the couch in the family room.

Jun pushed toys out of the way and stood Penelope on her feet, stepping back cautiously. "Alright baby girl, you got this."

He held his arms out to Penelope as she wavered on her feet, hands clasped together. Then she reached out toward Jun's hands and took a few cautious steps toward him. He backed away, a bright, joyous smile on his face as she continued to walk toward him. When she stumbled and began to fall, he swept her up, laughing victoriously.

"She's awesome! That was what, fifteen steps?"

Alena rolled her eyes, but her smile was pleased. "At least."

Still holding Penelope, Jun brought the wine over and refilled Valerie's glass. The smile he gave her should have been casual, but the look in his eyes spoke of more. Then he took Penelope with him and entertained her while he watched the game.

It was interesting seeing him in his element. Obviously comfortable in his own home, with friends, she learned, he had known since elementary school and college, she saw that the charm and humor was all genuinely who he was. She felt foolish for comparing him to Damien.

As she listened to insults fly from the men or played games with the boys, their eyes met on more than one occasion, setting butterflies loose in the pit of her stomach.

Alena leaned in and whispered, "It amazes me that no one has married that man."

Realizing that she had been caught, Valerie quickly looked away.

"Couldn't agree more. Val—"

She covered Maya's mouth, knowing her sister-in-law too well. "Please don't."

Alena blinked. "Oh. Ooooooooooooooh. I thought he kept looking over here more than usual."

Maya yanked Valerie's hand down. "She won't give him the time of day."

"Do you have 'Matchmaker' playing on an endless loop in your head?" She asked, thinking of the song from *Fiddler on the Roof.*

Maya laughed. "I do now!"

Valerie scowled as both women laughed. She rose from the couch and walked to the kitchen to throw her plate away.

Some of the lower cabinets close to the dining room had been converted into an enclosed space for composting, recycling and compacting. She was looking at it in surprise when Jun joined her. He was dressed casually in a gray sweatshirt with UW boldly printed across the front in black and black shorts.

So casual. So hot. It didn't make any sense.

"My alma mater is big on green and sustainable living. It stuck with me."

"That explains the hybrid, too"

"You noticed, huh?" He grinned, thinking less of the Lexus and more that she had noticed something about him.

Valerie ignored his question as she sorted her garbage. He had been successful in ensuring that she noticed him. And being alone with him in the kitchen, she was more aware of him than she would like.

That cocky grin paired with that relaxed stance reminded her of a cat who was about to catch his meal. Not ready to be caught, she left the kitchen, Jun not far behind her.

"I'm going to head home, take a break from sports. It was nice meeting you Alena. Dustin. Tony."

They waved and said their goodbyes. Much to her surprise, Jun followed her to the door and opened it for her while she slipped into her sandals. When she looked up, their eyes met and locked.

She had seen his blatant interest before, but the desire she saw there now hit her so hard that she had to bring a hand to her stomach to calm the butterflies. It was raw and honest, and nothing like she had ever experienced before.

Valerie realized at that moment that despite all her backpedaling and her fear of repeating past mistakes, it was only a matter of time before she gave in to what was building and boiling over between them.

Jun felt the air between them change and charge with their mutual desire. The easy smile that had been forming on his lips vanished as he felt the current strike him too. His eyes drifted down to her lips.

Was it his imagination or were they parted slightly in invitation? He lifted a hand –he wasn't sure why— and she bolted out the door, shouting out a strained goodbye before walking as fast as she could in her sandals.

A shout from behind him jarred Jun back to the present. He shut the door, putting what he hoped was a genuine smile on his face before he walked back and sat on the couch. He tried to get back into the game, into the conversation, but the same thought kept pulling him back.

What the fuck was that?

∞∞∞∞∞∞∞

Seriously. What the fuck?

Jun stuck his head back under the spray of water, trying, and failing to clear his head.

He couldn't stop thinking of the way Valerie had looked in that romper, the casual look so sexy that he thought it unfair, and looking at him like she wanted to undress him as much has he wanted to undress her.

Why had that moment of mutual acceptance of what was happening between them felt so life changing? This was all certainly a first for him, being so overwhelmingly attracted to someone who wasn't Asian, and with only words shared between them.

The chemistry was nothing like he had ever experienced before, and they hadn't even been on a date yet.

He shut off the water and scooped his hair out of his face, wringing it out lightly before pushing the shower door open. He yanked his towel off the rack and scrubbed it over his face, hating how he was feeling.

It was like they'd been two asteroids orbiting the attraction between them, but in that moment, they were viciously sucked in by the gravity of that attraction and were now on a rapid collision course headed straight toward it, and each other.

The idea of their bodies colliding was enough to give him a boner—god he wanted his hands on her—but he didn't like how out of control he felt. This whole thing was not anything like he experienced with a woman before, and he was pretty sure he fucking hated it.

She wasn't too thrilled about it either, he recalled

as he finished up his morning routine. He had never met a woman who was so actively determined to deny and avoid her own attraction.

There had been, of course, those who were absolutely not interested in him, no matter how thick he laid on the charm. But this situation? Completely new to him. It did interesting and terrible things to his ego.

Down in his kitchen, he pictured her in his space again. Lounging on the couch, laughing with Alena and Maya. Leaning on the counter, sipping wine. Frowning at his compost and recycle center.

He wanted her here again. As he began to scramble eggs, he wondered what he had to do to convince her to go out with him. Unfortunately, he had told her that she had the control here. He had been too focused on keeping his hands and mouth to himself to consider the ramifications of that decision.

Shaking his head, he turned on the news to distract his thoughts while he finished his breakfast and cleaned up after himself.

He was just about to get in his car when he saw hers drive by. Without thinking, he went out and over, walking behind the car as it pulled into the garage.

She stuck out a leg covered in red pants, that, he realized most unfortunately when she climbed all the way out, looked like they'd been painted on. It highlighted her toned legs and ass in a way that made him want to drool. She wore a matching sports bra that was a shade darker thanks to sweat. Her hair was pulled up in a tight bun so he saw the surprise that quickly registered on her face before giving way to caution.

You should be concerned, Jun thought. In that moment, he was convinced he knew how every bull felt when they saw that red cape, taunting it as it waved in the air. He wanted nothing more than to charge and devour her.

His hands fisted in his pockets as the heat that sizzled between them made its way straight to his groin. Fuck, this was pissing him off. The woman had done little more than smile and talk to him and he was reacting like a 16-year-old.

"Um. Hey, Jun. What's up?"

Why had he come over here? He couldn't think past the lust and frustration to remember what his purpose had been. Had he had one?

"Um, Jun?"

"I guess I just wanted to see if you were okay. We had a moment yesterday, and then you rushed off like I was the bogeyman." He pushed his hands through his hair in frustration, but since he had tied it loosely at his neck, his hair tumbled free. He was bending down to find the hair tie when he heard her sharp intake of air.

The way he looked up at her as he rose, with his hair tossed around his face, dressed in gray slacks, a pale blue shirt, and a boldly printed tie, he looked like an elegant yet wild lion about to pounce. His nostrils actually flared, as if he knew that there was a very strong possibility that the sight of him looking like that made her wet and he had scented her arousal. He took a step toward her.

"Jun, I—Wait—"

Without thinking, his lips swooped down to claim hers, silencing her. She was like fire. The taste of her burned his tongue and scorched his throat, leaving him thirsty for more. He burned where their bodies touched and the heat filled him, thawing out frozen places in his body that he hadn't known existed.

Had he always been this cold inside? Maybe. But with her, he was finally warm again.

The scent of her sweat surrounded him, and it gave him a bit of insight into what she would smell like after a night of passionate lovemaking. He wanted, more than he had ever wanted anything else, to take her to bed and make that a reality.

She had been about to protest, hadn't she? Her brain gave her no response. She heard nothing. Felt everything.

Something awoke inside her and shouted when his hands gripped her waist to pull her closer. Cheered when one hand left a searing trail of heat in its wake as it made its way up her body to cup the back of her neck, angling her head so he could deepen the kiss.

They both moaned when their tongues touched. Her hands dived into his hair, and he pulled her closer so that she felt the hard length of him against her. It was then that unreasonable panic swept in.

She shoved him away, had to check the urge to pull him back.

"Wait..." She held her hands out to keep him at bay. "Wait a second."

"Fuck me, Valerie. I feel like I've been waiting an eternity. Sloths move faster than you."

"I don't want—"

"That kiss says you do want."

God, she really did. "You need to leave."

"You're just going to pretend that you didn't feel that between us yesterday? That you didn't feel that just now?"

"Okay, so I felt something. And? So what?" She stomped to her trunk to yank out her gym gear, terrified that if she didn't keep her hands busy that she would put them back on him.

"We should—"

"Who gives a shit that you're fucking hotter than sin? I'm just supposed to fall at your feet when you beckon? Let you have your way with me like some sex slave? Fuck that noise. If you want to bully a woman into your bed, go pick somebody else."

She rounded on him now, eyes bright with righteous fury. "You want me? Fine. You'll get me on my fucking terms. Don't like that? Well, too fucking bad. Who knows how many women you've had waiting on the sidelines for your attention? Now it's your turn to suffer."

Her breath came out of a rush, her breasts rising and falling rapidly in her tight sports bra. His blood pooled in exactly two places: his face and dick.

Jun wasn't sure if he was more turned on or embarrassed. He had never been so rightfully put in his place, nor had he ever known anger to be so incredibly sexy. He was suffering all right.

He closed his eyes and took a deep breath. He wanted to pull her tight little body against his so she could feel just how much he was suffering. But he wasn't stupid, and he wasn't a caveman. Or at least he hoped he wasn't. He lifted his hands up slowly to signal he had enough and took a step back.

"You're right. You're absolutely right." He pushed his hands through his hair again and took another deep breath. "Look, Valerie, knowing you feel this crazy, visceral and raw attraction as much as I do is making me act like an animal. You don't deserve that.

I said I'd give you the control here, and I'm not handling it well at all. You're right—it is my turn to suffer. I am suffering. I guess I came over here to beg for a little mercy, but now I'll never look at the color red the same way again."

He left then. When he snapped out of whatever mindless zombie daze he had been in, he was in the parking lot of his office. Glancing at the time, he saw that he was thirty minutes late, but took a moment to ask the same question he had that morning.

What. The. Fuck.

CHAPTER 8

He avoided her.

It was likely she was avoiding him too, but Jun knew he needed to give her space. He had absolutely blown his chance with her like some pubescent tween with his first crush. This fact was made all the more embarrassing when he considered that he hadn't even taken her on a date. He didn't even have her phone number. Email. Facebook. Instagram. Nothing.

He was just the sleazy neighbor that had pawed at her.

And instead of moving on, he was obsessing over what she had said, on the charge that ignited when she stepped out of the car. On that kiss. It had blasted through him, leaving a hole he knew wouldn't be filled until he tasted her again.

He pissed her off, but she said that she thought he was hotter than sin. He believed that she wanted him and that she felt the attraction between them as keenly as he did, but she wouldn't be pushed or rushed.

He respected that, and would do a better job of showing that. Now that he wasn't being a prick, he realized that she was probably just as confused and agitated about this unexpected and all-consuming desire as he was. But instead of being patient, he had tried to force her to make the next move. To control her just as her bitch ass ex-boyfriend had.

He needed to devise a new word for pathetic and submit it with a picture of his face to whoever made dictionaries.

Since the new word evaded him, he used the weekend of the fiasco to go visit his parents in San Francisco. He told himself he deserved to hear his mother nag and scold him for being single after the way he had treated Valerie.

Then he had driven to Monterey and booked himself a room at his favorite beachfront hotel because he still wasn't ready to see her again.

For the first time in years, he had sat on the beach, watching the sun break over the horizon, and had felt the sharp pang of loneliness. Did he need someone to share these moments with?

His mother thought he did. She always said they would hold more meaning to him if he did. He never believed her, but he had wondered then. Wondered what it would be like to watch the sunrise with someone who meant more to him than someone who helped him pass the time.

It had left him feeling more than a little terrified when he started wondering what it would feel like to watch the sunrise with Valerie.

He knew then that it was time to step way, way back.

Over the next few weeks, he kept himself busy doing what he liked best—whatever struck his fancy. He copped tickets to a 49ers home game and spent the weekend in Santa Clara.

He popped over to Dustin's to watch a game or

dropped in briefly at Ruben's. He learned that if he kept his visit to thirty minutes or less, he could avoid seeing Valerie.

There had been a few wild Friday nights with Tony where they partied like they were in their twenties, only to remember the following morning that they were in their thirties.

It was one such morning when Jun growled in frustration as the doorbell rang incessantly. He lay sprawled on his stomach across the bed, still wearing last night's shirt, with his head bounding.

He reached for his phone and squinted at the light as he brought it to his face. Once he opened the Ring app, he saw Maya standing there, a determined look on her face as she rang the doorbell again.

"I'm sorry, Jun is currently dying right now."

"Jun better rise from the dead for Friendsgiving next week."

"Next week? I don't think—"

"Jun, sweetheart. Unless you know someone who is dying in the hospital right now, don't even bother saying you won't be there. Bring wine and mashed potatoes at two next week."

He groaned in response, and then winced when she rang the doorbell again.

"I'm sorry, that didn't sound like 'I'll be there'."

"Alright, alright. I'll be there."

∞∞∞∞∞∞∞∞

"You have to ask him."

"Nope," Ruben insisted, pulling a clean shirt over his head. "No man in the world wants to know if his sister…I can't even finish the sentence. Not going to happen."

Maya rolled her eyes as she settled the dress over her hips. "Your sister and good friend have been going out of their way to pretend they aren't avoiding each other."

"And obviously things didn't work out between them. Let it be, Maya."

"When they are in the same room for five minutes, sparks fly and we can pretend right along with them that it isn't happening, but it is. I'm tired of being singed, and Valerie needs to get laid."

Ruben plopped down on the bed. "I'm going to be sick."

"Oh, grow up." She straddled his lap, placing her hands on his face. "She's unhappy, Ruben."

He sighed, pulling her close to him. "So I'll kick Jun's ass."

"He's just as miserable as she is. Worse. His fake happiness is nauseating."

"It really is," he agreed, resting his forehead against hers. "But why does it have to be me?"

"You won't be alone in this. Alena is probably having this same conversation with Dustin as we speak."

Ruben chuckled, "You are such a meddler."

"And Alena and I will corner Valerie at some point tonight to ask her what happened."

"So you can ask Jun too. He's used to your bluntness."

Maya shook her head. "It'll surprise him more if it comes from you. It may surprise him enough to make the next move."

"Maybe. I kind of sort of told him about Damien. Could be why he's backed off."

"Oh, really? When did this happen?"

"A week or so after they met. He saw her at the grocery store and she got pissed when he tried to help her carry her stuff out to the car. I told him it was probably because she'd broken up with that controlling fuck face."

"Hmm. He doesn't want to come across as controlling, so he's waiting for her to make the next move. But since she's been running scared since the breakup that probably isn't going to happen."

Ruben hiked her dress up, hoping to distract her. "Definitely sounds like we should leave it alone."

Maya batted his hand away. "Wouldn't you rather have someone you trust help her find her backbone?"

"Yeah, sure. But Jun? I doubt he's looking for anything long term. We push them together now and we'll just be here again in a few weeks after he moves on to the next. So what's the point?"

"The point is, whatever happens, at least they won't be faking that there's nothing between them. It will just be nothing. Valerie may stop looking at every guy like he's the next Damien, and Jun may learn that once you go black, you don't go back."

"Ugh. I'm just going to go throw up now," he said, tossing her unceremoniously onto the bed before trudging to the bathroom.

"Don't take too long—everyone should be arriving soon!"

∞∞∞∞∞∞∞∞

Despite himself, Ruben paid closer attention throughout the dinner party. Maya had invited a few other friends, likely so Jun or Valerie didn't suspect a set up was in the works.

They sat at the dining room table, conversation flowing. He noticed that if you didn't sit back to observe—which was a hard feat in this group—it would be easy to assume Jun and Valerie actually talked to each other.

Oh, they might make a passing comment about something the other said, but mostly they threw themselves into engaging with everyone else. They pulled back if the other was drawn into the conversation, struck up a conversation with someone else, or left the table altogether under the guise of getting more food or drink.

Their eyes almost never met, and that struck him as outright bizarre. If Valerie looked at him, she looked just over his shoulder so what she was doing wasn't obvious unless you were paying attention.

But he had caught Jun looking at her a few times, and it made him wonder if that was how he looked when he had first met Maya. He saw a man wanting what was just out of his reach. Jun had masked it quickly each time, his gaze darting over to Maya to see if he had been caught.

It irked him a little to know that Maya was right. Ruben had to be the one to give Jun a kick in the ass because he wouldn't see it coming.

They spread out after dinner with some people leaving or others lounging in the family room or going for thirds. Ruben ushered Dustin and Jun to the backyard where they lit the fire pit and passed around cigars.

"I don't appreciate how my invite was delivered, but I am grateful for the invite. Your wife is an amazing cook."

Ruben chuckled. "You brought that on yourself, my friend."

Dustin leaned back in his chair. "What happened?"

"Remember I went out last Friday? Well I was more than a little hung over when Maya came by and just kept ringing the doorbell. If it wasn't for Ring, I would have actually had to go downstairs to tell her to go away."

Dustin laughed. "Serves you right for thinking you're 21 again. How come she didn't just text you?"

"Because you can say no in a text, which is what he'd done a few times when she invited him over to dinner."

"A guy doesn't want a second dinner and he incurs the wrath of another man's wife." Jun shot Ruben a glare. "You should be protecting me from her."

"Like I said—you brought that on yourself. You haven't been coming around, and Maya wasn't going to give you the chance to turn her down again."

"What's that about, I wonder." Dustin said.

Now Jun glared at him, knowing what he was hinting at. "Nothing. It just hasn't worked out."

"I have to wonder…" Ruben began, forcing himself to say the words. "Did you sleep with my sister?"

Jun's head whipped around to Ruben. "Are you serious?"

"You think I'd ask you that question if I wasn't?"

Dustin scratched his chin. "I've been wondering the same thing. You've been off lately. Figured it had to do with Valerie."

"I haven't been off. And nothing has happened between me and Valerie."

"Yeah so those two sentences can't both be true.

You've been off, and it's either because you slept with her or because you didn't."

Jun blinked over at Dustin. "I'm not having this conversation with Ruben."

"We gotta have it eventually. Might as well do it over a cigar."

Jun rubbed at his face. "You guys are insane. Nothing happened, I swear. I ran into her at a club one night." He couldn't, wouldn't tell him about their kiss. "There was a moment where maybe we both considered pursuing something, but then we backed off. Neither of us is interested in anything more. Happy? You got the whole story. Where's the lighter?"

"Right," Ruben said, checking his pockets. He pulled out the cigar cutter. "Forgot to bring the lighter. Mind grabbing it?"

"Yeah, sure."

Dustin and Ruben shared a look the moment his back was to them. When the door snapped closed, Dustin said, "Running scared."

"I was thinking the same thing. Takes me back to the day when I knew Maya was the last."

Dustin nodded. "Same. It's interesting that he's already turning tail and they haven't even started dating yet."

"Oh, god. Yet?"

"If Maya gets her way, it's yet. If they get out of their own way, it's yet. Either way, this shit is going to be interesting."

"Yeah, for you. As the brother and friend, I'm just going to stick my head in the sand and pray for it to be over already."

"Pray for what to be over?" Jun asked, closing the

door behind him.

"The game on Sunday," Ruben said casually, grateful for the opportunity to switch the topic to more comfortable territory, light a cigar, and forget this conversation ever took place.

Inside, Maya lounged on the couch with Alena and Valerie, pleased that her plan was going accordingly. With Jun outside getting his little nudge, she and Alena would give Valerie a much harder shove.

Completely necessary, she believed, since she knew Valerie was doing all she could not to attract Jun's attention in a long sleeve jersey dress that was shapeless enough to hide her figure. Oh she had dressed it up with enough jewelry so that it didn't seem overly obvious what she was doing, but Maya wasn't fooled, and she wasn't going to bite her tongue anymore.

"I can't believe Thanksgiving is here already," Alena shared. "Ugh, I do not look forward to holiday travel."

"I don't envy you, honey. How long will you guys be gone?" Maya asked.

"Tuesday to Tuesday. Jun, bless him, is taking Dustin's clients for that week so we can spend extra time with my family."

"Now if only Valerie would bless Jun with some extra time."

Valerie merely ignored Maya by sipping her wine and turning to face Alena. "Where are you guys traveling to?"

"Washington. What about you? Any travel plans for your Thanksgiving break? I don't remember how long elementary school breaks are."

"We have a kid free week, but I've got parent-teacher conferences scheduled for Monday and Tuesday. I've got nothing but R&R planned after that."

"You could plan a little R&R with Jun!" Maya suggested.

"I don't mean to pry," Alena spoke up before Valerie could. "But since we're talking about Jun and I have been seeing more of him than usual, I can't help but wonder what's going on between you two."

"Me too!" Maya sat up and pointed to Valerie. "I knew she'd make that face if I asked, so I've been giving her space and time, but now I want to know. It's obvious you two have been avoiding each other, so don't bother telling us nothing happened."

Alena at least had the decency to look sheepish, while Maya looked a little crazy around the eyes. "I have to agree with Maya. Jun has been different."

Valerie blinked in surprise, not expecting to hear that. "I don't know why. Nothing happened, not like you're thinking."

"I haven't seen you two since game day at his place, and it looked like he was ready to eat you alive. Tonight he's been stealing glances at you as if he's worried he'll get in trouble if you catch him. Something happened. We're just asking because we're worried about both of you."

Valerie sighed. "Look, I'll admit that there is a mutual attraction between us, but it was a little too intense and definitely too fast for me."

"Too fast? What did he do? Give me every single little morsel of details," Maya said, fanning herself dramatically.

"The day after the game, he dropped by right when I got back from the gym. I got the 'ready to eat you alive' vibe loud and clear. I was wearing the red outfit you got for my birthday, and he was the charging bull. He kissed me." She took a moment to sip more wine, unable to stop the words from tumbling out.

"I freaked. I felt that kiss down to my bones and I freaked out. Yelled at him. He apologized. He said 'You're right. I'm sorry' and then he left. We've been avoiding each other since. And it's fine, really. It's fine. I am obviously not ready for even a casual thing so it's perfectly fine that this is over before it even started."

"Wow, okay. Is it hot in here or what?" Maya fanned herself again. "You need to grab that bull by the horns and ride, girl!"

Valerie's mouth dropped open and Alena burst out laughing.

"Look, Valerie, I love you, but you are insanely stubborn. You should know that Ruben told Jun enough about Damien to keep him waiting for you to make the next move. You're treating Jun like Damien and unless I'm missing something, he hasn't done anything to deserve that. This is the last time I'm going to say this to you. Stop living in the shadows of your past relationship. Take back control of your love life. If you don't…well, the next party I plan to get you two under the same roof won't be as civilized as this one."

∞∞∞∞∞∞∞

Still unsure, and unable to settle down before bed, Valerie called London and Gianna to talk it through. But the conversation didn't go as planned.

"Wait, wait. You both knew about this?" Valerie asked.

"Oh, yeah," Gianna said, her cheeky grin so intense Valerie could hear it through the phone. "We helped set it up."

"Gianna and Maya did," London added.

"Oh and you were so against it," Gianna chastised.

"Actually, yeah, I was. You rush and push this between them and it could end badly."

"Ignore it, and it could end badly," Gianna argued.

"Cluster either way," Valerie interrupted.

Gianna rolled her eyes. "You two are so pessimistic."

"I think it's realistic," London said, her voice quiet. "I don't think you can be too careful when it comes to relationships."

"Pessimists. The both of you," Gianna insisted.

Valerie bit her lip, understanding that London's thoughts and feelings more closely mirrored her own because she had also been burned by an ex.

"Look, I'm team go for it, but not at the rapid speed that you and Maya are at."

"Agreed. But I feel like we're going in reverse," Valerie confessed.

"Duh!" Gianna shouted. "That's because you are."

"I have to agree, Val."

Valerie sighed heavily. "So what should I do? Ask him out on a date?"

"Yes! Absolutely!" Gianna cheered.

"How about just give him your number?"

"You two are killing me!"

Valerie smiled. "I like London's idea. I'll do it tomorrow. Will that satisfy you, G?"

"I'll take it!"

Later that night, she dreamt of drowning in shadows, and couldn't blame anyone but herself. She had taken the step toward Jun when she had invited him out that night, and then gone full reverse the moment she wanted to act on her attraction to him.

And that's where Maya had gotten it wrong. She didn't think Jun was anything like Damien, but she didn't trust in her own feelings because she had allowed Damien to manipulate them for so long. Her attraction to Damien had been instant, and he had preyed on her the minute he saw it.

She believed that if she allowed herself to feel such a powerful desire for Jun, just as she had with Damien, then she might someday ignore undesirable behavior.

That wasn't fair to either of them. She had to learn to trust herself again. She had to give Jun the benefit of doubt. And she had to be the one to fix the mess she had made between them.

Carrying her coffee tumbler and a piece of paper, Valerie made her way to Jun's and ignored the nervous tingling in her stomach. His garage was open and music was playing, and she knew that meant he was working out.

This was going to make things both easier and harder. For starters, it would be a complete role reversal from their last interaction in her garage, and if the man were shirtless, she would probably make a fool of herself. On the bright side, they would both have something to keep their hands busy. For her, at least, it helped her keep her thoughts organized when she was nervous.

Jun lay on the bench, arm muscles bunching and straining as he completed reps. The gray tank he wore was drenched with sweat and told her he had been at this a while. She recognized the song on the radio as something new and catchy instead of the rock music she heard the last time she had been in his space.

He caught sight of her when she leaned against the garage wall, but kept going until he finished his set. Since the music was blasting, she watched and waited. When he was done, he set the bar back in place before climbing off the bench to turn the music down.

"I just wanted to say something. I can come back later or get it out now while you finish up."

Jun took a sip of water, considering, and then thought it best to climb back on the bench so he didn't have to look at her. "Go ahead."

Valerie took a sip of coffee as he went back to his bench press. "I haven't been fair to you, and I'm sorry for that."

"You don't owe me an explanation, Valerie," he managed through heavy breathing.

She merely shrugged. "You're getting one. My ex was a dick, and I let him walk all over me. I have this knee jerk reaction to not let it happen again."

Yeah, he couldn't do this and focus at the same time, especially when she was pissing him off. He set the bar back down and pushed up again. "Don't apologize for doing what you have to do to protect yourself from dumb fucking men."

"But you haven't been—"

"Dumb?" He interrupted with a laugh. "I've been plenty fucking dumb in how I've handled things with you. Men are fucking dumb eight out of every ten interactions with women. It's coded in our DNA."

"Okay, but I think I haven't made it easier on you.

I've given you a lot of mixed signals."

Jun switched to a smaller bar to do bicep curls, needing to keep busy. "Nope. You want me. Bad. It freaks you out. The signal is pretty clear."

"Um...okay. Wow." She didn't know how to respond to his blatant display of confidence.

Now he grinned. "Sorry, it's the endorphins making me think clearly. Normally I have to use all my brain power to try to think past my attraction to you."

Since she was having a hard time thinking clearly herself, she took a couple sips of coffee to help her nerves settle. "Look, I just wanted to say I'm sorry and—"

"Your apology isn't wanted, needed or accepted," he said, his voice tinged with anger.

"I don't understand why you're mad."

Jun dropped the bar unceremoniously and snatched up his water. "I already told you. You have every right to want to do whatever you need to do to protect your heart, and it really pisses me off that you feel you have to be sorry for it. Don't. If you think I got too pushy, then I got too pushy. Say what you want to say, minus the goddamn apology."

Valerie gritted her teeth. "I just wanted to put the ball back in your court. I'm not going to pretend that I don't want this. I do, though 'bad' is a bit of a stretch. Here's my number." She moved forward and placed the piece of paper she brought on his bench.

He didn't hesitate. "Friday at six. Your ball."

"Seven. Your ball."

Jun rocked on his heels as he watched her walk away, a grin spreading across his face as he plotted his next offensive play.

CHAPTER 9

Jun convinced her to move their date up to 6:30, dropping small hints of his plans in text messages during the week. He kept it light as much for himself as for her.

It surprised him how much he was looking forward to going out with her, especially when he had been so sure that stepping back was the right course of action. Things with her were already unnecessarily complicated and it made him more than a little uncomfortable that part of him was too eager to care if it got more complicated.

Knowing that he was overthinking it, he avoided going over to the Halls that week. He deluded himself into believing that his decision made things better, not worse. The week was only going by so slow because people were already beginning to settle into the holiday lull with Thanksgiving less than a week away.

And he didn't perk up a little whenever he heard a car drive by or a car door close when he was working out in his garage.

When Friday finally rolled around, he was not, he told himself, a bundle of nerves.

Jun paired a moss-colored sweater with dark blue

jeans. He gave serious consideration to wearing his hair down, suspecting his date had a thing for long hair, but knew it wouldn't work for what he had planned for tonight. He opted instead to pull half of it back in a tight bun, and then headed downstairs where he filled his pockets with his wallet, phone, and keys. He slipped into black boots and tossed a gray coat in the backseat.

He parked his car in front of the Halls driveway and was rounding the hood when the garage opened up. Jun lifted his eyebrows when she stepped under the door before it fully opened and quick-stepped toward him.

"In a rush, Ms. Hall?" He asked with a grin as he opened the passenger door for her.

"I mean, if you'd like to answer Maya's—"

Jun cut her off by closing her door and running to the driver's side. He climbed in and started the car. "Say no more."

Valerie hit the button on the garage opener to close it just as the front door swung open. "Oh shit."

Jun laughed and waved at Maya as he drove off. "She's going to kill us."

"I told her you were picking me up at seven and begged Ruben to distract her at 6:30 so I could slip out. He'll be in the grave with us."

"Worth it," he said with a grin. "I've never had a date start off like an action film."

"Sorry to say it, but you'll never top it."

"There are about eight *Fast and Furious* films that lead me to believe I can."

Valerie rolled her eyes. "Ugh. You men and those movies."

"You men? What do you mean by you men?" He

demanded, feigning insult.

"Someone with an unhealthy attraction to fast cars, hot women, and impossible action sequences."

"Mmmm. Yeah, that's right."

Valerie laughed. "Do you need a moment alone with the car? You can pull over and I'll cover my ears."

"I think I can reign it in, but I may be up all night fantasizing about fast cars, a certain hot woman, and impossible action sequences."

The vibe shifted and the air charged so that it seemed that their attraction was a living, breathing thing that slithered and wrapped around them. His hands tightened on the steering wheel while hers curled into fists by her sides. The silence stretched on for a few miles before she spoke.

Valerie cleared her throat. "So, I assume we're headed to Roseville?"

"Yeah," Jun shifted in his seat and tried to ignore the scent of her perfume. "I figured there's probably a lot that's different in Sacramento and the surrounding areas since you moved to San Diego. I thought I might reintroduce you to your hometown."

She smiled at that. "You're going to show me my hometown? Where did you grow up again?"

"San Francisco."

"Wouldn't it make more sense for you to show me San Francisco and for me to show you around Sacramento?"

"Nope. You have to take me to San Diego."

"Ugh. Pass."

"Yeah. You. Me. Half naked on the beach. Definitely a pass," he took the exit, eased to a stop at the light. "That's why we're here in Roseville."

Valerie grinned over at him. "Are you obsessed with beaches?"

"Yes. Why aren't you?" He resumed driving. "No, don't tell me. I'm going to take you to my favorite beaches in the world and change your mind."

"Beaches? You have more than one favorite?"

"We'll start with low hanging fruit, like Hawaii, and then we'll go from there."

He continued listing off beaches in places she wasn't sure she had ever heard of while he searched for a parking space. Amused by his passion and impressed by how many places he had been, Valerie watched and listened.

This was the relaxed, confident Jun she had first met. He was in his element now, and it looked good on him. After a few rounds, he found a spot and then exited the car. He walked beside her and pointed to a restaurant with an expansive covered patio. He opened the door for her, and then checked them in with the hostess.

"Want to head over to the bar while we wait? It shouldn't take too long since I got on the waitlist before we left. I'm going to grab a beer."

"Yeah. Wine would be nice. Red."

Valerie looked around the restaurant while she waited. It had a casual and energetic vibe with lots of booth style seating. Large colorful canvas paintings covered dark colored walls. Judging from the bar, beer was king here, and they had several different kinds on tap. He was handing her the glass when the buzzer for their table went off.

"May I?" He asked when they were at their table, indicating her coat.

She sat her glass down before turning her back to

him so he could slide her coat off her shoulders. "If you tell me you do this with all of your dates, I'm calling you a liar."

Jun grinned and placed her coat on the seat next to her before taking off his own. "I'd hate to lie this early on, so all I'm going to say is that the man who invented chivalry is an evil genius."

Valerie angled her head in confusion. "Explain."

"Well, it's genius because each helpful act puts me a little bit in your personal space, lining up our bodies, stirring the scent of your perfume in the air. Then here comes the evil part because now my thoughts are veering off in a most inappropriate tangent, so please feel free to kick me—Ow!" He shouted, flinching from the pain. "Yeah, just like that because I promise you I deserved that."

"Settle down, Jun."

"Just give me a—Ow! Okay, okay. Appetizers. Appetizers. They have amazing truffle fries."

She smiled down at the menu. "I'm good with that. Why don't you keep things moving to the safe zone by telling me what makes Waldo travel so much."

Jun looked over at her, enjoying the way the pale pink blouse looked against her skin. "I'm lucky enough to have the time and the money, so why not? Day to day dentistry can get monotonous. Planning a trip or reminiscing about one helps me keep my edge, if that makes any sense." He paused to let the waiter take their drink and appetizer order. "Have you never used your breaks to travel?"

Valerie sipped wine, a little embarrassed by the truth. She had traveled a little—never too far—during breaks, but when things got serious with Damien, she had pretty much given that up just to ease his jealous mind.

Something on her face must have portrayed what she had been thinking because his expression darkened and turned a bit cold before he softened it again.

"When's your spring break? I'll take you to Hawaii."

"We're not even done with our first date. You can't say things like that."

"I just meant as friends, but if you're looking for a little—Ow! Damn, woman. That one was your fault, not mine!" He accused, rubbing his shin to ease the pain.

Valerie grinned. "You gave me pretty clear instructions to kick you. You practically begged."

"Oh, I am so going to kick your ass later," he scowled. "I was going to let you win because hey, it's our first date, but I will not show you any mercy."

"What are you talking about?"

"We're only in the second quarter of the game. I can't talk to you about the third. How was your week?"

She tried to get more out of him, but when he wouldn't cave, she told him about her week, the month. The school year. He was easy to talk to and seemed to be genuinely interested in the drama that was teaching third grade. She hadn't needed to kick him again for the rest of the night.

The fact that she was disappointed both baffled and confused her. There hadn't been any moments like there had been in the car or at his house. She should have been happy that she wasn't being smothered by sexual tension.

Instead, she was wondering where it went. He was

a perfect gentleman, and while she enjoyed it, she wanted to experience that animal magnetism again.

"Alright, we're going to have a brief half time," he said as they exited the restaurant. Instead of heading to the parking lot, he led her toward more stores. "I want you to think about how you're going to handle this ass kicking with grace."

Valerie stopped so suddenly when she saw their destination that he bumped into her. She stumbled forward a bit before his arms came around her and stopped their forward motion. His hair brushed past her face before he righted himself and she had a sudden urge to lean back into him, get a nice good grip of that hair, and pull his mouth down to hers.

"What? What happened?" He didn't let go, just turned her enough so he could peer down at her face. He saw her eyes flick down to his mouth and squeezed her shoulders in response to the sharp arrow of lust that blasted him straight in the chest.

"Nothing…I just…" *There it is,* she thought, *but now you can't think.* "I'm surprised you're bringing me to Dave and Busters."

Jun turned her so she faced him completely, his eyes hot with desire. "I'll take you wherever you want to go. Just not tonight."

He dropped his hands and forced himself to take a step back, and a deep breath. He walked around her to open the door.

"You've bruised my shin, and therefore my ego. Now I must make you pay by beating you at games, which, being a man, I will naturally be better at than you."

"Oh, really?"

"Yeah. Like I said, I was planning to let you win a

few, but you're going down."

They spent the next hour bouncing from game to game, and true to his word, he didn't go easy on her. She hadn't been above resorting to cheating by grabbing or tickling him in order to distract him. She knew it had the added benefit of turning him on by the hot looks he sent her or the way his lips went tight and thin.

Valerie had never had so much fun on a date before. It was entertaining, easy, and exactly what they needed after all the initial drama. Keeping it light and casual allowed them to start fresh, as if none of the drama had even happened.

At the end of the night, they pooled their tickets together and bought the biggest stuffed animal they could afford. Jun carried the pink and yellow polka dotted giraffe out to the car and opened the passenger door for her. He shoved the giraffe in the backseat before going around and climbing in the car.

"Okay, good choice," Valerie admitted, sending him a smile.

"Thank you. I must say, you handled that beat down with grace and dignity, despite playing dirty," he said pointedly, sending her a dirty look before backing out of the space.

Valerie merely grinned. "I have absolutely no idea what you are talking about."

"Go ahead. Feign innocence. I'll get even for that too."

"Promise?"

He swerved the car slightly and dramatically. "Woman, you're going to get us killed, making me think thoughts like that."

Valerie chuckled. "So, who has the ball now? What

quarter are we in?”

“Just started the fourth quarter. Tie game. My ball. Are we going to do this again? Your ball.”

“Yeah,” she said, taking a small breath. “We are.”

“Two points for me. What’s the first Saturday that works for you?”

“Probably the first Saturday in December.”

“How about dinner and a movie?”

She glanced over at him suspiciously. “I will not see another *Fast and Furious* movie.”

Jun laughed. “Got it. Why don’t you look up what’s out right now.”

They slipped into a quiet lull, which was broken up only sporadically as she threw out titles she thought he might be interested in. Jun saw that she was relaxed again, and wanted to keep her there. He could tell that those moments when their attraction came to the surface still unnerved her, and made her a bit skittish. He knew he had to keep it light from beginning to end.

So while he fantasized about pulling her into his arms and capturing that mouth with his for long, lazy kisses, he promised himself he could wait.

Besides, he wasn’t sure he could stop himself from going all the way if he kissed her again.

He pulled in front of her house moments after they settled on a movie and time that worked for them both. He climbed out of his car and jogged around to get the stuffed giraffe from the backseat. He walked her to the front door and stared at the Ring doorbell.

“Do you think Maya is watching?” He asked.

“Yes, yes I do.”

Jun grinned and handed her the prize. He took one

of her hands, held it in both of his as he brought it to his lips for a brief, soft kiss, his eyes meeting and holding hers. She saw that he wanted more, much more, and marveled at his ability to hold back.

"Goodnight, Valerie."

Then he took a step back, slid his hands in his pockets as he watched her. She unlocked the door and let herself in, waving to him before she closed it behind her. As Valerie walked to her room, she admitted that she had to give it to him. The man knew how to make a woman want to come back for more.

And she definitely wanted more.

∞∞∞∞∞∞

Between the simple fact that they were neighbors and Maya's meddling, Valerie saw Jun several times before their second date. Although, she wondered, as she applied makeup, maybe she could call tonight their third date. Or maybe it could be the fourth?

Maya hadn't done as Valerie had expected after their first date, so it had surprised her that she hadn't spent the entire Saturday giving Maya a play by play of what had happened. Instead, Maya had kept quiet the entire weekend, keeping busy with the boys and Ruben while Valerie prepped for her conferences.

On Monday, however, Maya made her move, and Valerie and Jun ended up sitting next to each other at the Halls dinner table. Maya had insisted that Jun was likely too tired from his day of seeing both his own and Dustin's patients to prepare a meal, and so she was happy to have him over.

The cheeky grin that Jun had sent her let her know

that he wasn't buying her logical explanation either.

At the end of the night, Valerie preempted whatever ridiculous plot Maya could concoct to force her to walk Jun to the door by simply doing it herself. Her heart rate had spiked the moment they were alone.

Again, he had looked at her like he knew the effect he was having on her. But he slipped into his shoes, opened the door, and said goodnight, his eyes trained on her lips until he turned to leave.

She had been a little disappointed that he hadn't kissed her that night, but then she had seen him on Wednesday… well that had been a little intense.

Jun had returned from a half day at work moments after she had returned from Thanksgiving grocery shopping. He came over and offered his assistance with unloading. Since Maya was out with the boys and Ruben was at work, she had gladly accepted.

She began unloading bags as he brought them in, and each time he went out, she became more aware that the house was quiet and empty. And that her bedroom was right next to the kitchen.

She wanted him there. Now.

He had been smiling when he brought in the last bag, but it vanished the moment he looked at her. He must have understood her intent, must have wanted her as badly, because he all but tossed the bag on the counter. It landed with a loud thunk that surprised them both enough to clear the lust filled haze.

They both froze mid step, realizing they had been moving toward each other. Then he said something and bolted. Her hands had been shaking when she closed the garage door.

Valerie sat on her bed now just as she had done

after he had gone. She had only seen him in passing after that, and she was okay with that. It was like they had made some unspoken agreement to chain their attraction to each other.

But the unintended consequence was that it just kept growing and growing, straining to be set free. She desperately wanted to break the chains even as she feared the consequences.

She placed a hand on her stomach to calm her nerves because she knew that if they were going to be able to function around each other, they had to loosen the chains.

She slipped into a black long sleeve midi dress that she found on an emergency shopping trip with London and Gianna that Sunday. She turned in the mirror for a better few of the zipper as she closed the dress, pleased with the way it accented and flattered her generous curves.

Glancing at the time, she pulled a large patterned scarf from her closet and tucked it in the crook of her arm. She gave herself one final spritz of the perfume he had commented on before, grabbed her purse, and strode from the room.

She waved to her family who were sitting at the dinner table, winking back at Maya with a grin. She opened the door, just before Jun could ring the doorbell.

His face went from surprised to happy and then to slightly stunned as he took her in. Valerie smiled knowingly even as she tried to calm her racing heart. Not yet, she thought, not now—but tonight, they would start to break the chains.

∞∞∞∞∞∞∞

Rein it in, Jun told himself as his thoughts took another nosedive.

He couldn't seem to think past the way she looked in that dress. When he had pulled her chair out for her to sit, his hands had actually itched to fill themselves with her perfectly shaped ass.

And the moment she sat, the scent of her perfume had wafted up to him and nearly made his eyes cross. He sat across from her, listening, but hearing absolutely nothing, and wondering, as he had been for the last two weeks, what it would be like to have her body beneath his, writhing with pleasure.

What the hell was he waiting for? She had made it clear that she was interested in letting him taste those luscious lips of hers again.

And he was almost certain that she put on tonight's outfit with the sole purpose of torturing him. Why the hell was he so hesitant to take things further?

"Jun."

He looked down when he felt the warmth of her hand on his. He turned it over to hold it and bring it to his lips and tried not to think of where else he would like to kiss her. He put on what he hoped was a convincing grin as he looked back at her.

"Yes?"

"You seem awfully distracted tonight."

Now he grinned for real. "You forgot to kick me."

Valerie watched as he startled and froze when her foot slid up and down the inside of his leg. "No, I didn't."

His hand tightened on hers for the briefest of moments. "Ah, so I was right. You are trying to torment me."

"I think you're confusing torment and seduce."

Holy shit, he thought, and blinked at her in surprise, watching a sly smile spread across her lips.

"Am I? That'll be a first," he said, giving her a playful smile as his heart raced. "I guess I was too busy thinking about how to seduce you to pick up on it."

"Yeah, I don't think that's what was going through your head."

He just looked at her because she was right, and he couldn't share the X-rated thoughts he had.

Valerie laughed. "That's what I thought. Your restraint is impressive. I wasn't expecting it," she added after a beat.

Jun chuckled. "I know I haven't been on the best behavior since we met, but I found my patience. Am I moving too slowly for you now, Ms. Hall?"

"No, I…" She paused, trying to find the right words. "It just feels like I'm in a pressure cooker when we're together."

The moment the words left her mouth there was a change in pressure in the air around them. They stared at each other for what seemed like minutes before he started to clear their tables.

When he came back, she looked over her shoulder at him. The intent she saw there made her knees weak.

He took her coat and helped her back into it before leading her outside, his hand tightly gripping the fabric at the small of her back. Valerie couldn't decide if she was walking faster because he was or vice versa, but she was grateful when they reached the car.

Jun walked her to the passenger side door and rounded on her, giving her a small push that had her falling against the car. She looked up at him in surprise, her breath catching before he crushed his mouth to hers.

He pressed into her, desperate to feel the shape of her as he devoured her. Some inner voice warned him to slow down, to be careful. But when she wrapped her arms around him, her mouth hot and eager on his, the voice became nothing more than a slight buzzing in his ears.

Valerie couldn't breathe. She didn't want to breathe if it meant pulling away from him. The chains were loose, and the beast broke free, pawing at her body, grabbing her ass, pulling her close enough to feel how ready he was to take her.

Knowing that she elicited such a genuine and reckless reaction in Jun was the most exhilarating moment in her life. Greedy for more, she slid her hands into his hair and grabbed fistful to change the angle of the kiss.

She was rewarded when his tongue dipped past her lips and swept into her mouth to play with hers.

Her tight little body was wreaking havoc on his, robbing him of all rational thought, and stealing his breath. He couldn't breathe, and he couldn't stop tasting her.

So he swallowed her moans, and gripped her ass tighter. He needed to get her naked, needed to bury himself in her heat. He lifted her, moving to the right.

They bumped into the side view mirror of his car. He stopped then, broke the kiss and looked around. Breathing heavily, he remembered where he was.

He looked down at Valerie, saw that her eyes were

soft with desire and her lips were swollen from his as she too struggled to catch her breath.

"Holy fuck," he said, putting her back on her feet.

Valerie slumped against the car. "I'm just…just going to stand here for one second."

When he tried to step away, her hands tightened in his hair and guided his mouth back down to hers. Gentler now, their lips brushed and pressed, retreated and came back for more. They were dizzy when they finally pulled away.

Jun rested his forehead against hers, fighting for calm. That had been…devastating. But only because he was so raw with need from putting that kiss off for so long. Yeah, that's exactly what it was. It only felt like that because they had both been denying themselves the opportunity to act on their attraction to each other.

He took a deep breath, feeling relieved by his logic. "The lesson here is don't wait so long to kiss me next time. All that bottled up sexual energy turned you into quite the animal."

Valerie snorted out a laugh and felt any remaining tension leave her body. "Oh yeah, that was all my fault. I'm so sorry. Are you okay?"

"I'll live. Could use a beer though," he added. "Thank god you can choose your seats at the movies."

"We're still going to the movies?" She asked in surprise. He had brought her to the car so she had just assumed he was taking her home.

He grinned, pulling her with him toward the theater. "I just needed a relatively private space to release the pressure."

Delta Shores was a newer shopping center, built

from the ground up just off a freeway exit that hadn't existed when she had lived in Sacramento. Restaurants ranged from quick dining to fast food. When they'd driven in, she had seen a large display of major retailers.

She imagined it would take an entire day to hit up all the shops. They had opted for poke for dinner, and the restaurant was within walking distance to the movie theater. He got them both a beer and carried it to their theater, trying to look relaxed.

She both admired and hated his restraint. It took her a minute to get into the film because she spent the first fifteen picturing herself straddling him in that seat. She didn't understand how he could be so nonchalant when he had nearly destroyed her.

She allowed herself one small moment to doubt that he hadn't been as affected as she had been before she squashed it. He had lost control. She all but heard the moment the reins on it had broken.

He wanted her, but had still insisted on going to see a movie when all she could think about was how hard he had been when he had pulled her against him.

Valerie was quiet on the drive home, and replaying their kiss in her mind, imagining how it would feel when he touched her for the first time. When she heard the car door open, she sat up, found Jun standing next to her and her house behind him. She blinked up at him.

"Did I fall asleep?"

Jun smiled gently, helping her out of the car. "Yeah. Let's get you inside."

"Ugh, I'm sorry," she said, yawning.

Jun stopped at the end of the walkway and pulled her into his arms. "Don't incinerate me this time."

Valerie smiled sleepily up at him and slipped her arms around his neck. "I can't make any promises."

He brushed his lips against hers gently, and then pressed them briefly against hers. Then again. And again. And again, until she thought she would go mad. Then he moved them over hers slowly, tasting and pressing gently.

Each time she tried to increase the pace he changed the angle, kissed just the corner of her lips until she settled down again. She melted against him in surrender and said his name on a plea.

He pulled back then, fought for control. "Go get some sleep, Valerie."

"Walk me to the door," she whispered.

Jun took a step back. "And get caught on camera with a massive boner? Pass. That's why I stopped here. Go inside."

"Why?"

Jun closed his eyes, understanding what she was really asking. "I need you to go inside, Val."

He didn't open them again until he heard the front door open and close. He walked back to his car, drove it the extremely short distance to his house and garage, then closed the garage, turned off his car, and just sat there for a moment trying to wrap his head around the idea that maybe he was just a little bit afraid of how much he wanted her.

CHAPTER 10

He slept like shit, of course.

He took a cold shower, hoping to get rid of the massive boner that had prevented him from walking Valerie to do the door.

When that hadn't helped, he had been left with no choice but to handle it, and if Valerie knew the fantasies he had concocted around her to help him handle it, she probably wouldn't want to see him again.

Then he laid in bed for the next few hours, tossing and turning, wondering why the fuck he was in bed alone when she had made it perfectly clear that she had wanted to handle his boner problem.

But when he had seen that she had fallen asleep on the short ride home, he had known work and the holiday had caught up with her. Even though it had taken all his strength to let her go, he believed his future self would thank him later. He wanted her to be well rested when he finally got her in his bed.

He didn't know what time he had finally fallen asleep, but he had only been able to sleep until eight.

His head was pounding, his stomach growled, and he felt like the walking dead.

When the doorbell rang, he gave serious consideration to murdering whoever was at the door. He opened it and after seeing his sister there, thought of ways to dispose of her body.

"What are you doing here?"

Mika lifted an eyebrow before pushing past him. "Making you angrier, obviously."

She sat on the bench, pulling off her boots, while Jun scowled down at her. "Obviously. What do you want?"

Mika dropped on his couch and looked at him critically. "While I think I may need to start worrying about your memory, *ojiisan*, I suspect your current foul mood and inability to use your brain means you didn't get lucky last night."

Jun didn't know if he was more annoyed that she had called him grandpa or that she had been spot on about the cause of his mood. He rubbed his hands over his face, trying to clear his head.

"I literally just woke up. I haven't had food or coffee."

"And you're grumpy because you didn't get laid. I tried to tell you to date outside your little Asian only box."

Jun visualized wringing her neck and dug down deep for patience. "Mika. Did you need something?"

"Man, you really are losing your memory in your old age." She leaned forward and spoke slowly, enunciating each word. "You are dropping me off at the airport. I brought you my car. You are taking it to get detailed so we can give it to mom and dad for Christmas."

Jun plopped on the couch next to her, rubbing his face again. "Fuck, I did forget. Your flight leaves at 10, right?"

Mika rolled her eyes. "Yes, and thank goodness I have pre-check. It's eaten up quite a bit of time trying to get your brain working again."

"Sorry. I've had a lot going on. And yeah, I need to get laid."

"Ugh. Gross."

"You brought it up. You mind brewing me a cup of coffee while I put myself together? You know where the k-cups are."

"Fine. Hurry up. I'd rather hang out at the airport than here with your hormonal ass."

Jun rushed upstairs and into his bathroom. While he brushed his teeth, he yanked a sweatshirt from the closet and then pulled a comb through his hair to give it the illusion of tame. Mika was putting her shoes back on when he came down.

The Keurig finished dripping in his tumbler as he approached. He brought it to his lips and took a few sips, nearly groaning in satisfaction as some of the fog in his brain began to clear. Then he popped the lid on, grabbed it, and walked out with his sister.

Mika's little Nissan sat in his driveway. He was just about to open the driver side door when he heard a car start over at the Halls. Jun turned to see Valerie backing out of the garage.

"Give me a sec," he told Mika before making his way down the driveway.

Valerie saw him as she backed onto the street. She stopped the car in front of his driveway after he waved to her and rolled the window down. She wondered why he looked just as good in a pair of sweatpants and a sweatshirt, his hair wild around his face, as he did last night in his button up and jeans.

Then she noticed the petite Asian woman watching them curiously, and wondered who she was.

"Hi," he said.

"Are we about to have an 'about last night' type of conversation?"

Jun laughed. "No. I just...I don't know what, actually." He just wanted to see her, but wasn't ready to admit it out loud. He leaned over so only she would hear him. "But maybe we can have that convo another day. Saturday night maybe?"

"Maybe." Valerie leaned toward him. "Why are we whispering?"

He brushed his lips over hers and the rest of the fog cleared as desire shot straight through him. He knew he was in trouble when a woman tasted better than coffee.

Valerie sat back, shaking her head with a small smile. "Real slick."

Jun grinned. "See you Saturday."

"Yeah, yeah. Uhm, Jun."

"Yeah?"

"Who's that?"

"Who?" Still grinning, he turned toward his house and when he saw Mika gaping at him like a kid on Christmas morning, he stopped. "Ugh, my sister, who

I completely forgot was there. I gotta take her to the airport. I'll catch you later."

Valerie grinned and waved to them both as she drove off.

Ah, fuck, he thought and stomped to the car.

Mika all but bounced in the car. "Oh my gosh oh my gosh oh my gosh! How long has that been going on?"

"Calm down!" He demanded, backing out of the driveway, and winced when she squealed in excitement. "Jesus, you're like one of those insane little yappy dogs."

"I can't believe you actually listened to me for once."

"You get that idea out of your head. You had nothing to do with this."

"Oh, yeah right. I tell you to date an African American woman at our cousin's wedding and bam—here you are, a few months later, making kissy faces with one!"

"Not how that happened. I was already thinking about it before you brought it up."

Mika rolled her eyes. "Whatever, who cares. All that matters is that you've finally broken out of your predictable little mold. What's next?"

"We've only been on like two dates."

"And you're definitely going to see her again. I can't believe it!"

"Whatever. You can't say anything to mom."

Mika looked over at him in confusion. "Why would I say anything to her?"

"I don't know. Just don't, okay?"

"Oh, damn. You're serious about this chick."

"I didn't say that."

"And yet," she said thoughtfully, "You brought up *kaasan* as if gossiping about your love life is something I do often."

Caught, he swallowed the lump in his throat. "So then just drop it."

"Nope! Are you thinking mom is going to freak when she finds out?"

"There's nothing to find out."

"That's a yes. I wouldn't worry about it."

That wasn't what he was expecting to hear. Actually, he wasn't sure what he was expecting to hear, but he knew it wasn't that.

He told himself to drop it, to ignore her until he could think it through. He lasted a full two minutes.

"Why?"

Mika smirked. "Oh, no. You've taken my advice without giving me my due. No more free advice for you. You go to the source with that question, and wonder what I know until then."

He scowled at her. Ignoring him, she launched into conversation about her travel plans. He didn't listen. Couldn't.

While she talked, he wondered why he even mentioned their mother. He and Mika never talked to each other about their personal lives, and she seemed to know that if she did know about a woman he was dating at any particular moment, then it was just that. A moment.

Mika never had any expectations of meeting any women he dated, and so she wouldn't even have anything to talk about with his mother.

He decided to let it go, not wanting to stress about it if he couldn't come up with a logical answer. He had a date to plan, and this time, he didn't plan on sleeping alone when it was over.

∞∞∞∞∞∞

Tonight was for romance, and Valerie experienced a side of Jun that she hadn't expected.

He escorted her from the front door to the car, his oversized umbrella protecting her from the winter rain, as he helped her inside. Since it was pouring by the time they arrived at their destination, he used the valet and had insisted she wait for him to come around with the umbrella.

He chose a small Italian restaurant with low, ambient lighting, hushed music, and intimate dining tables for two.

Candlelight flickered between them as they exchanged stories about their favorite holidays and family traditions.

She learned that they sat on near opposite spectrums when it came to Christmas, with her on team Christmas, which she hotly insisted was the sane side. She talked about her plans for Christmas break and he talked about places he hoped to visit one day.

He had kissed her softly and sweetly, one hand holding the umbrella, and the other pressed to her lower back to keep her close while they waited for the valet to bring his car around.

She had insisted on connecting her phone to his car and now that they were on their way back, she used the ride home to sing her favorite Christmas songs while he complained of pain and torture.

When he slowed to a stop in front of her house, she reached over and pressed the garage button she had found while connecting her phone. Their eyes met before she settled back into her seat.

He put the car back in gear and drove it into the garage. Parked, he looked over at her, his eyes hot with unspoken desire, while his hand hovered over the button.

She watched him, waiting, and held her breath until he finally pressed it. It took her a second to realize that the rumbling she heard was the garage door closing and not her heart hammering against her chest.

They climbed out of the car, stood in front of his door to slip out of their shoes. After he unlocked the door, he held it open for her, and then followed her into the kitchen.

Her breath caught when she felt his hands on her shoulders. He slid the coat off, tossed it on the counter, and then did the same with his own.

Jun tugged at her hand, held it while they went upstairs to his bedroom. He led her to his bed and turned on one of the side table lamps so that soft light filled the room.

They dove at each other the moment he turned around. Mouth to mouth, they fumbled with each other's clothes. Why had he worn a button up, Valerie wondered as they both struggled to undo the buttons.

Then he was flinging it open even as she shoved it off his shoulders. Her hands cruised down his chest, and across his abs, and she moaned at the feel of him as they made their way to the snap on his jeans. He shook himself out of the shirt just as she unzipped him.

He groaned against her mouth before shoving his hands under her sweater, pushing it up until she lifted her arms to help him get it off. He turned her and pushed her down so she lay on her stomach.

Straddling her legs, he leaned down to press his lips against the small of her back. She moaned in response, writhing beneath him and making him harder. He flicked his tongue over her spine, enjoying the little whimpers of pleasure she made, before he unclasped her bra.

"Jun," she panted, trying to turn over. He was driving her crazy, and she couldn't even touch him. "Let me—"

"Not yet," he interrupted, standing so he could turn her over.

She removed her bra as he undid her pants zipper, then let out a breathless laugh, as he started yanking none to gently in an attempt to get them off. She pushed her jeans and underwear over her hips and then lifted her legs, helping him pull them off.

She started to sit up, but he was on her again, pressing his lips to her neck as his hands found her breasts. She wrapped her arms around him as he teased her body, making her dizzy with pleasure.

He wanted to feast on her all night. From head to toe and back again. And the sounds she made when he lapped at the curve of her neck. How could he stop when she made those sounds? Hungry for more, he trailed his fingers down her body until he found her center.

"Oh god," they said in unison.

He dropped his head to her chest as he touched her gently, marveling at how wet she was, how she responded to his gentle strokes. When he brushed his thumb over her clit, she dug her nails into his shoulders.

"Fuck me," she groaned.

Jun wasn't sure if that was a command or a curse, but his control snapped in response. Blind with desperation and a need that threatened to overwhelm him, he pushed off of her and yanked open the drawer where he stashed his condoms. As he ripped open the packaging, she pushed his pants and boxers over his hips and down his legs.

Her hands gripped his hips and turned his body toward her as he slipped the condom on. His dick came tauntingly close to her mouth, and for a second he pictured that succulent mouth taking him in, but then she scooted back on the bed and lay down.

Settling between her legs, Jun braced himself over her with one hand and used the other to rub his cock against her, nearly coming then and there as he coated it with her juices. He put just the tip in and leaned over her, burying his face against her neck before he slid home.

She wrapped her legs around him and shoved her hands into his hair as he rocked into her.

Dizzy from the scent of her perfume and their lovemaking, Jun closed his eyes against the spinning room and pressed kisses against her shoulder. The urgent goal met, he kept his pace slow and steady, stretching out the pleasure as long as he could.

When she slid her hand down between their bodies to find her clit, he knew she must be close.

He needed to see the moment she fell apart. He pushed up and grabbed her hips, pulling her with him as he moved toward the edge of the bed. Placing his feet on the floor, he gripped her hips and resumed his slow pace, his eyes watching her face.

She pressed and stroked her clit, unraveling before him. He felt her clinch around him, and then she let loose a desperate moan, her back arching up off the bed as the orgasm ripped through her.

Jun lost it then. His nails dug into her hips and he pounded harder and faster, riding his own orgasm out before he collapsed on top of her. Barely holding himself up on his forearms, he slowly recovered. As his breath returned, he grinned against her neck.

This is what he had needed all along. All the unnecessary stress and drama, overthinking every interaction with her. Now that they had finally done something about their attraction to each other, he immediately felt like himself again. Not only that, he had that same level of calm satisfaction he got after coming home from vacation.

And wasn't that interesting, he thought, as he felt Valerie shift under him, trying to get comfortable in the weird position he had put them in.

Jun shifted his hips so he slid out of her, digging his hands into the bed when she groaned in response, the sound igniting fresh desire. He stared down at her face a moment, wondering how that was even possible.

Fresh scratches on either side of her hips caught his attention as she scooted back further on the bed. It confused him when he felt equal parts pride and horror.

"I…uh…guess I got a bit rough there at the end," he brushed his fingers along her hip where he had marked her.

Valerie lifted up on her elbows to see. "I guess you did."

"Will you stay and let me make it up to you?"

She tilted her head, considering, as she took open stock of his body. He was leaned over her slightly, arm muscles tightened and bulging as a result, and his ponytail was in such complete disarray that his hair was a mess around his face.

She could just make out the six-pack that she had the pleasure of touching when she had helped him with his shirt. Then she dropped her eyes to his crotch, and thought of everything she wanted to do to his body.

"I think I can do that."

∞∞∞∞∞∞∞∞

Valerie woke to soft light filtering in from the drawn blinds and the sound of Jun's quiet breathing behind her. She rolled over to face him and found him lying on his back, hair spread wildly over his pillow.

He had thrown the comforter off his chest and hips, drawing her gaze over his naked flesh. Her blood began to hum with desire as she remembered just what the man was capable of.

She guessed it to be about six in the morning, and she wanted to pounce him as though they hadn't spent the night wearing each other out.

Oh, they had taken time for other things. She had curled up against his side, listening to him recount his travels as he told her about the places in the photos that covered his walls, and was impressed that he wasn't half bad with a camera.

He had taken her into the kitchen for snacks, and after they had finished eating, he had made her into his own personal snack before they finally made it back to his bedroom.

It had disappointed her a little bit, since she suddenly found herself looking forward to having sex in the kitchen for the first time, but she had been much more comfortable taking a bite out of him with her knees on his carpeted floor than she would have been on the kitchen tile.

Despite the brief snatches of sleep he allowed her, Valerie felt energized. Knowing she wasn't going to be able to go back to sleep, she slipped quietly from the bed. Grabbing her clothes from the floor, she tiptoed to his master bath, gently shutting the door behind her so she could get dressed.

When she was finished, she eased open the door and found the bed empty. She made her way downstairs and saw Jun standing in front of the Keurig.

He turned when he heard her coming, giving her another view of his washboard abs and inadvertently making her drool.

"Want some coffee?" he asked when she was near him.

Valerie shook her head. "Figured I'd get a cup at home after I grab a shower. Sorry if I woke you."

"Don't be," he said, pulling her to him. "Are we going to do this again?"

She smiled, liking that he asked the same way he had after their first date. "I've got plans Saturday, but Friday night will work."

"Oh, Ms. Hall," Jun said gravely, his face portraying his disappointment. "I'm afraid that's the wrong answer."

Before she could question him, Jun turned her around, pressed into her so she could feel how hard he was. Last night he had lifted her up onto the counter on just this spot so he could eat her out, but now he wanted to do what he hadn't. He placed the condom on the counter in front of her, nipped at her ear as his hands went under her shirt to cup her breasts.

"Take off your pants," he demanded.

Heart racing, Valerie unsnapped her jeans while his lips and hands wreaked havoc on her body. He knew where to touch her now, knew that flick of his tongue at the curve of her neck made her weak with pleasure.

He pushed her bra up, rolled her nipples between his fingers with just the right amount of pressure that made her cry out his name. Hands shaky, she pushed her pants and underwear down.

Before she could step out of them, he pushed her down and held her in place as his other hand trailed down across her ass and eased between her legs where she was already wet for him.

Jun stroked her with a finger lightly, gently, and then placed two over her clit. Mercilessly, he rubbed and stroked her into a frenzy before easing the fingers inside her.

Because he hadn't allowed her to step out of her pants, she couldn't spread her legs. The position made her tighter than she had been when he had played with her before. He couldn't get past how hot she looked right now leaning over his counter, ass perked up while his fingers eased in and out of her.

Valerie moaned, trapped and needing more. The counter was cold, but her body was on fire. She couldn't think past the pleasure, only knew that it somehow wasn't enough. Then he was pressing the condom into one of her hands.

"Open it," he commanded, shoving his shorts down and kicking one leg out.

Valerie obeyed, held it out toward him. "Hurry."

Jun rolled the condom on. "That's the right answer." And eased into her.

So tight, he thought, squeezing his eyes shut against the pleasure that threatened to overwhelm him. He focused instead on the keening sounds she made, on the way she cried out.

He had never met a woman who said fuck, both commanding and cursing him as he did just that. It made him never want to stop, never want to feel anything other than how he felt when he was inside her.

Then he looked down and watched the way her ass jiggled when his flesh slapped against hers. The contrast of their skin made him drive into her harder and faster. She reached down the way she did, rubbed her clit.

"Fuck fuck fuck!" He shouted as they came together.

Jun placed his hands on either side of her on the counter in a poor attempt to keep his weight off of her. Pressed against the counter, she admitted that was probably the single hottest fuck of her entire life and she would likely never look at his kitchen, or any kitchen the same ever again.

His hands came up to rest gently on her hips before he pulled out. She wasn't sure how he had the ability to move, but she couldn't find the strength. Even when he tugged her panties and pants up her legs she didn't lift herself off the counter.

"Valerie."

"Hmm?"

"If we're going to get your pants back on, you're going to have to help me a little."

"I'm good right here."

Jun knew she was pretending, but the idea that he had fucked her senseless inflated his ego and made him want to do it all over again, especially if she didn't move from that position in the next two minutes.

Baffled that he could want her so soon, he gently eased her up, turned her in his arms.

She looked at him through heavy lidded eyes. "I think I'll take that coffee now. To go. I really do need a shower."

"I have a few showers here," he said, turning to retrieve a mug from his cabinet.

Fixing her clothes, she considered the offer. She was picturing shower sex, her eyes far away, when he pulled her toward him.

"I can see where your dirty little mind is going, and I approve," he said, lifting her up and starting toward the stairs.

Valerie laughed and wiggled out of his grasp. "You are insatiable."

"Says the woman who was picturing me fucking her in the shower," he responded, stepping toward her.

"No. No," she tried again, more firmly when a grin threatened to cross her lips as she backward away from his advances. "Jun, we can't have sex all night and all day!"

The devilish smile that spread across his lips made her stomach drop.

"Challenge accepted."

And then he snatched her up.

CHAPTER 11

He freed her at noon after proving her wrong in the shower and only really because he had run out of condoms. There had been a moment when she considered telling him that she was on the pill, but she squashed that thought just as quickly as it formed.

They had only been on a handful of dates, and even though she had known him for almost three months now, it was entirely too early in whatever the hell was happening between them to take such an intimate step forward.

She didn't care how great the sex was.

Thinking she could sleep for a week, Valerie let herself into her brother's house. She could hear her family upstairs and didn't feel the least bit ashamed when she rushed to her room.

She gave her phone a cursory glance and saw that she had several missed calls and text messages, most of them from London and Gianna. Not ready to deal with that just yet, she stripped and put on her robe.

Despite the shower at Jun's, she didn't dare call herself clean. They had done some really dirty things in the shower she recalled, strolling smugly into her bathroom. Her shower sex experience had been quite limited, but she was sure now that Jun had plenty practice there.

She had balked at getting her hair wet, warning him that her dreads would take time to dry with just a hand dryer. He had responded to her concerns by showing her his height adjustable showerhead and had kept his promise of keeping her hair as dry as possible with some very interesting positions.

So she got clean for real this time with a quick shower. After toweling off and wrapping up in her robe, she stepped out of the bathroom and into her room.

Then shrieked in surprise when she found London, Gianna, and Maya on her bed.

"Oh my gosh! You're all right! We were so worried," Gianna said, jumping up to pull her into the room and shut the door.

Valerie didn't believe that for a second. "Oh, please. You expect me to buy that bullshit?"

Caught, Gianna grinned. "We expect every little detail."

"Can I get dressed first?"

"Don't let us stop you," Maya said, batting her eyes at Valerie.

London held her arms up when Valerie looked at her with pleading eyes. "Don't look at me. This is completely your fault. You didn't respond to our text and calls, and you call that insane woman your friend. There's nothing I can do for you."

Valerie scowled as she stomped to her closet. "Oh and I suppose you had nothing to do with this?"

London gave her a gentle smile. "It was hard to say no when she showed up at my door at ten am."

"What the hell have you been doing for the last two hours?" She demanded, pulling on a fresh pair of underwear.

"Shopping at Target until I texted them that you were here. Stop stalling. Spill!"

Valerie tossed her robe aside, pulled a dress on over her head, sat in her desk chair, and spilled.

"Holy shit!" Gianna exclaimed. "Holy shit. Why didn't anybody tell me to get an Asian guy?"

London rolled her eyes. "I did."

Gianna glared at her. "Surely you didn't."

London merely shrugged, knowing that Gianna liked to pretend that her ex never existed, which would mean that she didn't actually have firsthand experience dating an Asian guy.

Understanding that that was a sore topic, Valerie tried to switch gears.

"Ethnicity has nothing to do with how great a guy is in the sack."

Gianna slanted her a look, unconvinced. "Oh really? So Damien wasn't better?"

"Nope. Not even close. I mean, they both knew exactly what to do, where and how to touch. But with Jun…His intent was what made all the difference."

Curious, London leaned forward a bit. "How so?"

"Damien was an expert lover, there's no other way to put it, really. But after being with Jun, I realized that Damien was an expert lover so he could brag about it. He was always just a little bit smug after we had sex, like he knew he'd blown my mind and would spread the word about his sexual prowess. Thinking about it now, I don't even know if he actually enjoyed the sex"

"That's fucking fucked up, Val," Gianna said, her voice low with anger.

"Right," she breathed, a little embarrassed to admit it. "But Jun? I'll go ahead and give him the title of expert lover, but I don't think for a minute that he's working for that title. His intent was to enjoy every fucking minute of getting off and getting me off. I've always enjoyed sex, but this was on a whole other level that I didn't know about."

"When are you going back over there?"

Valerie's mouth fell open. "Geeze, Maya. I liked it, but I'm not a machine. I'm pretty sure we've had enough sex for one day."

"Fair enough. When will you see him again?" London asked.

"We might go out on Friday. I didn't confirm it before I came home."

"I am just so excited that you're dating again!" Gianna squealed.

Maya stood to leave. "Well, honey, you ride that bull until he can't go no more. I'm going to go have my way with your brother, so you gal's keep an eye on my boys."

"Oh, my. That just happened," London said, blinking after Maya as she left.

"Is she serious right now?" Gianna asked.

Valerie's shudder was the only answer they needed.

She took them all out to lunch in penance. Though Natomas boasted two In and Out restaurants, both were packed. They crammed into a booth and waited for their food. Valerie caught up on her text messages while London and Gianna entertained her nephews, grinning the entire time.

She had a couple of emails so she went through those too and found another from Claudia about Damien.

To: Mallorie Smith

From: Claudia Newman

Subject: Happy Holidays

Your ex is a fucking psycho! We learned this the hard way, but seriously, I think he's escalating!

He sent you two letters here, one from him and one that says it's from the alumni association. I bet he assumed they would automatically be forwarded to you or I would mail them to you. Hah! Nice try, fuckwad!

With your previous permission, I open any mail that comes for you, which is hardly anything, so of course this got my attention. In the letter addressed from him he goes on about how much he misses you and begs you for his forgiveness and for you to come back to him and that he'll change and never do it again blah blah blah bullshit bullshit. Nobody cares or believes that trash!

The "alumni" letter though? Had a fucking Tile tracker in it! He is gung ho on finding you, Rie. I really think you need to consider coming back and filing that restraining order. I'm going to keep this garbage just in case you change your mind, but I really do think it's time. Let me know, chicka.

- C

Fuck, she did not want to deal with this crap. She had what felt like a really healthy and mature relationship for once, with a man who was amazing in the sack and treated her with the utmost respect.

She just wasn't ready to go there yet and instead chose to believe that with time, Damien would move on. But she shot back a quick email, thanking Claudia for giving her the heads up and telling her she would get back to her with a decision.

Then she put it away and committed to enjoying her friends and family.

∞∞∞∞∞∞

It was February when Jun realized he might be in a relationship.

He stepped into the reception room at his office and gaped at pink and red hearts that Evelyn had proudly displayed on the walls throughout the room. She decorated for nearly every holiday, always putting her decorations up on the first Monday of the month.

She never deviated from that tradition, so unless there was a new holiday that he didn't know about, it was February.

Jun sat at his desk and pulled up his calendar, then stared at it as he tried to figure out how the month had snuck up on him.

Christmas dinners and New Year celebrations had kept both he and Valerie busy for several weekends, making date night all but impossible. Valerie had stayed a few nights during her two-week winter break, and that had been the most he had seen of her during the holiday season.

It was almost mid-January when their schedules had lined up again, creating an opportunity for them to go on another date. Had he seen her every weekend since?

He thought back, recalled the night he had taken her to The Kay, a downtown district of Sacramento named for its location on K Street. Restaurants, bars, clubs, and other entertainment venues lined both sides of the street and were accessible via light rail if driving or taking a ride share wasn't an option.

They had dinner at a Mexican restaurant and had the pleasure of experiencing a live Mariachi band. Then they had walked down to Dive Bar to reminisce on the night when things between them had started to shift.

Another weekend they had gone to the drive-in. Valerie had marveled at the renovations the site had undergone, and they had fogged up the windows on more than one occasion. This past weekend, they had kept it simple and gone out for pizza near home.

Holy fuck, he thought, not sure what to do here. He never dated women from January fourteenth to Valentine's Day.

It was a rule he had set for himself while getting his PhD when there had only been time for fuck buddies. Enough of those buddies had started expecting more right around Valentine's Day to spark the habit of taking those thirty days to avoid dating or sleeping around. He realized now that he had never quit the habit.

Until now.

Not only was he dating, he had been seeing Valerie exclusively for almost three months.

He needed a second opinion, and briefly considered bringing it up to Dustin before deciding he needed to hear from another perpetual bachelor. He wasn't sure a man who was happily married could be brutally honest. Rose-colored glasses and all.

He sent a quick text to Tony instead, asking him to meet for a beer after work. Tony would give him the cold-hearted truth. Thankfully, he was free, but now he had to get through the rest of the day.

Despite struggling to focus, he made it. As soon as he was done with his last patient, he checked out and walked down to Malt and Mash Irish Pub. He ordered two beers, then sat staring at them while he waited.

"You look like you're going to be sick."

Jun looked up at Tony and hoped he wouldn't be. "How would you describe me and Val?"

There was a moment on Tony's face that spoke volumes, but just as quickly, he averted his gaze as he sat.

"Friends with benefits?" He inquired, trying to sound casual.

Jun scowled at him. "That's not what your face said. And that was a question, not an answer."

Tony looked up at him, face carefully blank. "I don't know what you're talking about."

"Tony, seriously."

"What? Friends with benefits. Isn't that what it always is?"

"Yeah," he answered quietly. "It is. But you don't think that's what is going on."

Tony shrugged as he drank. "What I think doesn't matter."

"You know it does."

He sighed, debating what he should say. Jun hadn't had anything resembling a real relationship for as long as he had known him. It wouldn't surprise him if Valerie ended up being the one to change that.

Since he had his own reasons for feeling that way, he had taken a step back ever since Maya had stepped in to push them together. He wanted to let their relationship run its course without further interference.

"I think you know the answer. If I say what you don't want to hear, you will just pretend it's just hormones or convenience or whatever. So if you want to know what I think, you're going to have to be straight with yourself, and with me. Take some time, think about how you want to answer that question and get back to me."

Jun leaned back in the chair and thought back to the day he first saw her, and the five months that followed.

They had a date this weekend, and he was looking forward to spending time with her, looking forward to having her in his bed. He wasn't ready to end it yet. Did that mean he was ready to take it to the next level?

∞∞∞∞∞∞

He was acting weird.

Valerie glanced over at him while he drove. Jun hadn't been his usual, playful self throughout dinner. There'd been snatches where it had come out, but it still paled in comparison to his normal behavior.

He had been just a little bit distant, as if he was sorting out something in his mind that required so much of his attention and focus that he couldn't concentrate on what was happening right in front of him. She was worried that she understood exactly what was on his mind.

Valentine's Day.

She had zero expectations for the lover's holiday, but given his behavior, she was convinced that he thought she did.

The assumption that all women loved Valentine's Day was annoying, and knowing he bought into that stereotype as well kind of pissed her off. She didn't need or want more from him than hot sex when their schedules lined up.

She was content to keep it casual and didn't want things to get weird between them just because some commercial holiday said she should be dreaming of diamond necklaces, candy and engagements.

Fortunately, she had planned for this. She had hoped for Plan A, where they carried on like it was any other day, but now saw she had to implement Plan B.

Pulling out her phone, she shot a quick text to London and Gianna to let them know that they would have a Galentine's weekend sleepover instead of just Galentine's Day brunch.

"Hey, so there is this sushi place in Arden that the teachers are raving about. They said something about how the sushi comes to your table on a conveyor belt."

Jun smiled over at her. "I know what you're talking about. They're pretty good."

"Would you mind if we went?"

"Yeah, sounds good."

"Sweet. I'm booked pretty much every weekend except for the 29th. I figure Saturday would be better since getting to Arden from Natomas will be a headache on a Friday night."

"Sure, that sounds—" Jun cut himself off when he realized she had skipped to the end of the month. Right past Valentine's Day. "The 29th?"

Valerie nodded, smiling over at him as if he wasn't looking so deeply confused. "London, Gianna, and I are going to have a Galentine's Day weekend next week, and then the week after that, I'm meeting with a realtor to look at some condos."

"Wow. That's a lot. Let's start with the only part I actually understood. You're moving?" What was this feeling that was settling at the bottom of his belly?

"Eventually, yeah. You didn't think I planned on living with my brother forever, did you?" She laughed at the idea.

"No, of course not. Ruben mentioned that you were saving up, I just didn't think it'd be so soon."

"I thought the same, honestly. But moving up here didn't cost as much and I paid off my student loan sooner than planned, so I've been saving a lot of money. Then my parents surprised me at Christmas with twenty-five thousand dollars. They opened term savings certificates for Ruben and I when we were little, and just kept rolling the funds over and so it would continue to build up until we needed it for something like this. With what I have in savings, I have enough for a down payment on a condo in the $250 thousand range. So, I'm going to see what I can get for that in Sacramento. If I don't like what I see, then I'll wait."

"I'd wait," he said, and not because he suspected there was a small part of him that didn't want her to move.

"That's what my realtor said," she pouted.

Jun nodded. "Sounds like you got a good one then. What was the other thing you said? Gal day?"

"Galentine's Day," she corrected. "It's an unofficial holiday on February 13 where ladies get together to celebrate their friendships. Have you not watched *Parks and Rec*?"

"Uh, nope," he admitted. "What do you do on Galentine's Day that requires an entire weekend?"

Valerie shrugged, hoping he was asking out of curiosity and not because he wanted to do something on Valentine's Day.

"It's been a while since we've gotten together. I've been busy doing other things." She slanted him a look to indicate she meant him. "We plan to have a night of movies and booze at London's, brunch the next morning, and end it with a shopping spree at the Galleria. If you don't hear from me on Sunday, know I'm likely still recovering."

"I'm picturing naked pillow fighting." Jun parked his car in the garage and tried to cover up what he was feeling with humor. "Text me pics."

Valerie rolled her eyes and climbed out of the car. "No way. Besides, I don't think I can sleep with you again until you've watched Parks and Rec."

He turned to send her a look that made her just a little bit wet. "Wanna bet?"

"Sex, sex, sex. I'm talking about the national treasure that is *Parks and Rec!*"

"I want to park and rec that ass," he said, tugging her upstairs.

She nearly collapsed with laughter. "That's the lamest thing I've ever heard."

"Yeah, but since you're going to be gone the entire weekend, you better believe that's what's happening tonight."

Jun shoved her up against the door and crushed his lips against hers. He ordered his hands to be gentle, but they moved like they had a mind of their own, pulling her dress up and over her head before yanking the cups of her bra away to free her breasts.

He leaned down, scraped his teeth over one breast and grabbed a greedy handful with the other. He nipped and sucked at her nipple, knowing he would leave a mark. He wanted to leave a mark so that she would see it and think of him.

Mad with desire, Jun dropped to his knees and jerked her leggings down her legs. She had gotten smarter, he thought wildly, and had dressed knowing where they would end up. Knowing he couldn't wait to get her naked.

He would show her how grateful he was that she thought ahead. She had just barely stepped out of the leggings when he fixed his mouth on her, his tongue lapping at her as her hands grabbed fistfuls of his hair for balance.

Valerie struggled to remain upright as he ravished her, turning her inside out with pleasure. He lifted one of her legs and then the other so that she was balanced precariously on his shoulders.

It gave him better access to her clit, and he took full advantage, flicking his tongue against it, matching the movements to the pace he set when he slipped two fingers inside her. She cried out, writhing against the door as he pushed her closer to the edge. Suddenly terrified of the fall, she tried to push away.

"Oh, fuck, Jun— I…I can't! Please. Let me—"

"You will," he ordered, his fingers moving faster. "You will. Let go. I've got you. Let go."

"Oh god!"

He didn't let her fall gently, but kept fingering her and licking at her clit until her screams died down to a weak moan and he felt more of her body weight against him.

When he placed her legs down, her knees buckled. He caught her, placed one hand under her legs to lift her up and into his arms. He carried her to the bed then laid her gently across it.

Whatever beast had ripped through him had quieted, and was replaced with a need so fierce it hurt. Jun stripped off his clothes, took a condom from his drawer and ripped it open.

As he pulled it on, he watched her lift up enough to unclasp her bra before collapsing back on the bed. He climbed on top of her, bracing himself on his elbows so he could see her. Her arms slipped around his shoulders and tangled in his hair to pull him down for a kiss.

Gentle now, he slipped inside her, kept his movements slow and deep while they kissed. She tasted every moan, felt every shudder that wracked his body as he fought to keep the pace. When he was close, he broke their kiss, struggling to breathe as he rested his forehead against hers. She pushed his face up so their eyes met, held him there.

"Let go," she whispered. "I've got you. Let go."

"Ah, fuck. Valerie."

He tried to bury his face in her neck but she held him steady, watching as the orgasm tore through him. He held her gaze, moving inside her until he was empty.

Weak, Jun managed to fall to his back. She curled into his side, pulled the covers from the opposite side of bed over them. With her hand resting over his racing heart, he stared at the ceiling until he felt her drift off.

Ok, Jun, he thought. *It's just you and me.*

He heaved a huge sigh, searched for the name of the strange emotion that he had felt before he batted it back with humor and replaced it with angry lust.

Oh, there it is, he thought, feeling the burn of it in his belly now that he was too tired and exhausted to feel anything but the hurt that sat there like a heavy weight.

She had hurt him.

He had been prepared to take things to the next level and ask her to be his girlfriend on the most cliché day of the year, and she had made other plans.

And instead of just talking to her, he had kicked that little emotion in the balls and took out his frustration through rough sex. Ultimately, he really didn't care about Valentine's Day. That wasn't the issue.

As he listened to her quiet breaths and felt the comforting warmth of her body, he realized he probably should consider that maybe they didn't want the same thing out of this relationship.

CHAPTER 12

They toasted their Galentine's weekend with a bottle of wine London had picked up in Napa Valley. After they finished their first glass, London turned on *Parks and Rec*. While it played quietly on the TV, they set up trays of food on the little beat up coffee table in the middle of the living room.

Valerie sipped contently, her feet propped up on an ottoman, as she surveyed London's ever-growing collection of toys and figurines. Her studio apartment was located in the heart of downtown Sacramento, and what it lacked in size, London made up for in personality.

From Star Wars to basketball to a shelf overflowing with books in the three languages she spoke, the space was loud in a way that London never was.

London had always been the quiet one in their little trio. Not shy, or introverted. She was the quiet beauty who was just a little bit uncomfortable with the attention she received because of her looks.

Perhaps that was why she preferred to constantly observe and soak up her surroundings. It gave her a reprieve from the attention. Valerie always thought, however, that the behavior was one of the reasons why London had been incredibly successful at learning many different languages.

She may not show all of who she was to the outside world, but being inside of London's apartment, she knew the space truly reflected the unique and interesting person that she was. Valerie was grateful that she had such an amazing and multifaceted friend.

"You ever consider moving? I'm concerned you have more memorabilia than clothing."

"No." London smiled around a bite of cracker. "And you're probably right."

"Don't waste your time trying to talk sense into her, Val," Gianna suggested. "Our friend is dead set on downtown living."

London stretched out. "I haven't had a car payment or paid for gas in almost three years."

"I'd say I'm jealous, but I like having a car. You could stay downtown and just get a bigger place."

London shook her head. "I'd just fill it with more collectibles. Plus, this place is rent controlled. I'd probably end up paying double the rent on this place for only two hundred extra square footage. I'm good here."

Gianna swirled her wine as she stared at it. "I think I'm going to buy a place. Not anytime soon. Probably two or three years from now."

"Really? But you love your place in Folsom."

"I do," she clarified before finishing off her drink. "But I can feel the beginnings of this little itch between my shoulder blades."

"There are creams for that," Valerie said with a grin. "It's been a while since I've heard you say that. You used to say it every fifteen minutes in high school.”

“Ugh. She really did. So annoying.”

Gianna grinned. “Such is the life of the young and the restless. But yeah, it’s been a while. I’ve been in the same job and in the same house for almost seven years now. At ten, I’m thinking it’s going to be time to make some moves.”

“As someone who just moved from San Diego, I feel that.”

“And speaking of moves,” Gianna sat up and reached for the platter to spread pepper jelly and cream cheese on a cracker. “I can’t believe you ditched Jun. I appreciate it—chicks before dicks and all that—but I could really use some dick and I so don’t appreciate you passing up on some.”

London laughed. “What she said.”

“Ugh. I thought we weren’t talking about men tonight.”

“You wish. I was just waiting until you got a little sloppy before I brought him up.”

Valerie scowled at Gianna. “You are the worst best friend ever.”

Gianna merely reached over and refilled her glass.

“I think it’s smart to pull back. You don’t know how his parents feel about interracial dating.”

Now Gianna scowled. “I forgot that getting you sloppy meant you might find some way to bring up that douchebag. Can we not? He is so last year.”

London waved her chicken wing at her. “You know I’m right. Not everybody’s parents are cool with interracial dating.”

“You’re both making this a bigger deal than it is. So is Jun. I’m not ready to take things to the next level with him, and I especially don’t want to do it because of some dumb holiday."

"Because of Damien," Gianna said.

"No—"

"You haven't had enough wine if you're sticking to that lie."

"And just for that, I'm not drinking anymore." Valerie stuck her tongue out and sat up to pile her plate with finger foods. "Seriously, G. Not tonight. I'll think about all of it when the weekend is over. Right now, I just want to enjoy my besties."

Gianna pouted, but she let it go. Valerie, on the other hand, struggled to keep her thoughts from veering back to Jun.

Would she have approached her relationship with Jun differently if things hadn't ended the way they had with Damien? Was she using Valentine's Day as an excuse to keep from forming an emotional tie to Jun?

She knew that if she told she them the truth, the whole truth, then they might be able to help her make better sense of what she was feeling. But she was sobering up now, and without booze to drown the embarrassment and shame, she couldn't bring herself to let the words out.

∞∞∞∞∞∞

Jun decided to give himself over to the pleasure of her company rather than give in to the urge to push her into talking about why she really ditched him on Valentine's Day. She obviously wasn't ready to define their relationship just yet, and he had to accept that. For now.

So he took her to his favorite ramen spot in

Japantown a few weeks later. After they placed their order, he pulled out his phone and logged in to his credit card rewards account.

"Like I said, I definitely have enough points for the both of us," he said, showing her his phone.

Valerie shook her head, refusing to look. "It doesn't matter. I can't save money to buy a house and go to Hawaii."

"Actually, you can. The flight is only $200. You're telling me you can't spare $100?"

She gave him a look that spoke of her disbelief. "How is that even possible?"

Jun stood and joined her on her side of the booth, draping his arm around her to pull her close. He again held his phone out. "Look. I didn't use any of my points when I went to Crete, so I've got a good balance. I put in your spring break dates, and it shows me how much two round-trip tickets to Hawaii would cost after it uses my point balance. $243.52."

"But you're saving those points," she said, looking up at him. "I can't let you waste them on me."

"Stop being ridiculous. It's not a waste. You haven't taken a vacation in eight years. You deserve one, and using my points won't break your budget."

She bit her lip. It wasn't just the cost she was worried about. "What about the hotel?"

"Since I'm a huge snob, I tend to stay at all-inclusive resorts. They can be pricey, so I'll pay for that. Don't argue," he insisted, when he saw that she was going to object. "To make it a little more fair, you can pay the entire $243 for our flights, and I will accept kinky sexual favors as repayment for using my points."

She shoved him away. "Ew. You perv."

He chuckled, going back to his seat after the waiter set down their bowls. "I told you I'd take you to Hawaii. What kind of friend would I be if I didn't keep my promise? Think about it, but you need to let me know by Friday."

"What, why?"

Jun rolled his eyes. "You think you're the only one on spring break? We wait much longer and everything will be booked up or be more expensive. Hell, we're lucky that flight is even still available."

"Fine," she said, thinking about it now as she dove into her delicious bowl of ramen.

It wasn't the cost that concerned her, not entirely. It was the little spark that ignited in her belly the minute he had talked about commandeering her spring break.

She had forgotten that he said he would take her to Hawaii, and honestly hadn't believed he had meant it when he said it the first time. She had only mentioned her spring break to tease him when he said he needed another vacation.

But a vacation together? That was something that couples did.

They never talked about what they had, operating instead on the unspoken agreement to see each other exclusively. And she had convinced herself that she was content with the status quo until he started painting a picture of them lounging together on beaches.

Now she was starting to realize she wanted more from their causal relationship.

She had balked at the idea a month ago, but planning for the upcoming weekend and planning for the near future changed things in her head. If they were willing to save a place in each other's lives beyond right now, that meant something more was happening here. And she wanted more. She wanted to see where this would take them, and she wanted to be on the same page.

She couldn't help but take a deep breath. She had never felt this way with Damien. He had never given her a chance. Anything and everything she felt for him was just a reaction to something he did or said. It was a bit scary to know that these were her true feelings, and not the result of some convoluted seduction or guilt trip.

After they finished eating, they meandered through Japantown. The indoor and outdoor shopping space was home to an assortment of sushi, ramen, and shabu-shabu restaurants and dessert spots.

Gift shops and stores sold Japanese fashion, goods, and other specialty items. The 5-tiered Peace Pagoda stood proudly, beckoning guests to lounge around and drink in its beauty.

Jun led her to a local market where they could purchase grocery items imported from Japan. They wandered around the store while he pointed out some of his favorite childhood foods and snacks.

"Jun?"

He turned, found his cousin standing there. "Hey! What's up, Alex!"

"Hey, man. What are you doing out this way?"

Jun nodded toward Valerie. "Just showing my girlfriend around. Val, this is my cousin, Alex. Alex, Valerie."

Valerie's eyes flew to Jun's and then back to Alex when he stepped forward to shake hands. "Hi. Nice to meet you."

Alex grinned. "Same."

"What about you? What brings you here?"

"I took my parents to look at some appliances—they finally agreed to let me replace their 1980's rat traps. And of course mom wanted to stop over here. She's right over there."

"Oh, yeah? I better go say hi." He glanced over at Valerie. "Do you mind?"

She shook her head, unable to form any words, and watched him walk away. Alex said something, speaking what she had to assume was Japanese, which made Jun stop in his tracks.

He cast a tentative glance her way, a blush creeping up his neck while Alex continued to grin, obviously amused to call Jun out on his slip. Then they rounded the aisle, leaving her alone with her thoughts and emotions.

A deliciously warm feeling settled in her heart. She liked that his thoughts were headed in the same direction as her own. She liked that in the recesses of his mind, he had already staked his claim.

But she wasn't just his possession. He had said my girlfriend with pride, as if the title meant he had won a great prize. She liked that. A lot.

Jun made his way back to Valerie, and then stopped to watch her for a moment. She had paired a loose gray sweater with dark blue jeans and white tennis shoes. Her dreads were straight now and looked longer since they weren't curled.

She's mine, he thought, and realized then that he couldn't put aside his desire to elevate what they had anymore. He wanted people to know that he was hers. He needed her to be his.

Maybe she wasn't ready yet, but he wasn't going to

let it go this time. He moved toward her, determined to make the title stick.

"So I may have given my cousin the impression that you're my girlfriend." When she jumped in surprise, he placed his hands on her shoulders. "And possibly my aunt."

"And me," she reminded him dryly as he led her out of the store.

"Yeah, yeah." No going back, he thought. "So, I didn't correct them," he said, stopping to face her on the street. "I mean by now she's probably told my mom, and Mika already saw us together so convincing them otherwise would be a colossal waste of time. So. You're my girlfriend. Do you think that is going to be a problem for you?"

She blinked up at him, waited for the flutter of butterflies to settle in her chest before she spoke. "I think you're asking me the wrong question."

He brought his hand to his chin and scrunched his face up as if in thought. "Oh. Right. Now that you're my girlfriend, it's not a big deal if I pay for the entire trip to Hawaii. But would you agree that you should still repay me in kinky sexual favors?"

Valerie had to grind her teeth together to keep from smiling, especially when he grinned and closed the space between them. He placed his hands on her hips, and leaned down to brush his lips gently across hers. She bit his lip in return. The butterflies took flight again when his grip tightened and his eyes went soft with desire.

"So that's a yes to the sexual favors, right?"

∞∞∞∞∞∞∞

He gave her a little preview of what he had in mind when they got back to Sacramento, then reluctantly kissed her goodbye a few hours later.

Since she had to prep for school, it gave him the opportunity to make the call that had been on the back of his mind since he made his Freudian slip.

"*Ohayou, kaasan.*"

"So, you have a girlfriend. When can I meet her?"

Jun blinked, surprised that she got straight to the point. "It's a little early for that, mom. We just made things official, you know?"

"Oh," she said, the disappointment evident. "I thought this was the same woman you were seeing in October."

"Yes, but—Wait. No. I mean…we weren't. How did you…" he trailed off, completely confused.

Ayaka chuckled. "You dropped by last October and sat there silently while I nagged you about settling down. Since those are two things you never do, I assumed there was a woman."

"I don't know what to say."

"So it is the same woman."

"Yes. Valerie. She's…" he paused for a moment, sighed a little. "She's black. I know you wanted me to be with a Japanese woman."

"Yes, but—"

"I really don't think it's a big deal. At first, I guess I did. I thought we might be too different, assumed our cultural values would be so different that it would be too hard to make our relationship work. But it's not like that. Or at least it hasn't been. I don't think it will be."

"You've given this a lot of thought."

He took a deep breath, realizing he had. "I guess I

have."

"Then let me ease your mind. I have friends whose children have chosen a partner their parents didn't approve of. Some have come to accept their choice; others have completely cut them out of their lives. Some are happy, other's hide their misery. I choose to be happy."

Jun hadn't realized he was carrying that weight until it fell from his shoulders.

"*Arigatou, kaasan.*"

"So, when do I get to meet her?"

CHAPTER 13

Weeks later, Valerie made the realization that the title didn't change the dynamics of their relationship, and much of what did change she attributed to their preparations for their vacation together.

She had insisted that they stop going out as much in order to save up money for the trip. Jun, whose career didn't come with the same financial constraints, rolled his eyes at her suggestion, but went along with it.

As a result, they got together more often during the week for dinner and spent the weekends streaming TV shows and movies.

The weeks had flown by, bringing them to this day in what felt like the blink of an eye.

Valerie looked over at Jun. He was dressed in khaki linen shorts and a blue shirt, and had tamed his hair in a tight bun that sat on top of his head. The casual look suited him and his easy, relaxed mood. He was chatting animatedly with their Lyft driver, his hand resting lightly on her thigh, completely at ease.

Was she crazy for thinking this trip was a big deal? She had gotten to know a lot about Jun since they had started dating, but she couldn't help but feel a romantic vacation upped the stakes in their relationship.

They were essentially going to be living together for an entire week. From this point on, they would spend every waking and sleeping moment together until they went their separate ways when they got home next week.

What would she learn about him? What little habits did he have that would only make themselves known in situations just like this?

She knew she was borrowing trouble, but couldn't help it. This was entirely brand new to her. There had been times when she had stayed at Damien's place for a week, and he at hers, but this felt different. There had been a slight lack of intimacy and connection with Damien the longer she had been with him.

She had been too emotionally exhausted and damaged to do anything more than keep up the facade of their relationship. She had chosen the easy way, so that by the time she had been brave enough to call things off, she didn't feel anything for him anymore.

But with Jun, there was so much intimacy and connection. It was there in the way he rested his hand on her thigh, or the way he would glance at her occasionally, as if he was letting her know that nothing ever had his full attention when she was around because part of it was always on her.

It was there when he kissed her and when he moved inside her. It was so much more than what she had ever experienced before.

This trip would bring them closer, and she wasn't sure if she was unsure of where it was going, or if she was terrified of where she thought it might be heading.

Valerie didn't know if she was making sense, so she forced herself to shift her focus and enjoy herself. They were booked on a direct flight to Hawaii that promised to have them there in just less than six hours. Because they had booked so late, they ended up having to purchase Hawaiian Airlines extra comfort seats, which she had translated to extra expensive.

Still, thanks to Jun's points, the total had only risen to $540. The six hours would be spent in a little more comfort than the economy seating.

"Where'd you go?" Jun asked, as he pulled her bag from the trunk.

Valerie dragged it to the sidewalk. "The beach. You talked it up so much that I'm already picturing myself there."

Jun grinned at her before taking her bag and pulling it along with his own to the ticket counter. "You're going to love it."

They checked their bags and made their way up to security. This was no quiet Saturday morning. The airport was alive with activity, with people rushing or meandering to the people mover that would carry them from landside to airside.

On the ride over, she managed to convince Jun that he didn't need to suffer with her by going through regular security since he had access to an expedited security line. It took her nearly three times as long as it did him to get through security, so when she met him on the other side, she understood why he opted for it.

When they met on the other side, he took her hand and led her to the gate. "We're right on schedule. Flight boards in twenty."

"Wow. I didn't believe we'd have enough time."

"That's the beauty of Sacramento. It's just the right amount of busy. And living ten minutes from the airport doesn't hurt either. I've done this enough times to know exactly how much of that recommended two hour window time that we actually need."

"I'm happy to leave you in charge from here on out. Of travel," she added when she saw the way his eyes lit up with mischief. "Pervert."

"There's the water," he said with a grin, pointing to the filtered water station. "I'm going to empty the tank while I still have elbow room."

They arrived at their gate with their water bottles filled and their bladders empty just as the airline announced that boarding would start soon. As they boarded the plane, the reality of the situation hit him.

He had a girlfriend, and they were going on vacation together. The first was a rarity, and the second was a first. But as he watched her as she took in her surroundings, a small smile playing across her lips, he was excited to be embarking on a new adventure with her.

Jun spent the first part of the flight regaling her with stories about funny flight attendant announcements, passenger mishaps, and painful flight experiences.

When their in-flight meal arrived, they were famished, and devoured it within minutes. Then she curled into his side while they watched a movie, and dozed off just before it ended.

He stared down at her as she slept and gently caressed her cheek. This was the more his mom had spoken of, he realized, his heart beating quickly. He had a strange, sinking feeling that he would never be the same after this.

∞∞∞∞∞∞∞

Valerie was whisked away within minutes upon their arrival at the resort. Jun's down to the minute planning included a two-hour spa experience for her immediately after they checked in.

The massage bed sat on a raised platform of gleaming dark wood. Two wooden cabinets in the same material stood prominently against the wall and it was there she was directed to place her clothing and don the robe that was inside.

Once undressed and snuggled up in the soft, silk robe, she sat in the lush armchair on the other side of the room and placed her feet in the bowl beneath it. The therapist returned and drew open the blinds and door, letting in the beautiful Hawaiian light and smell for her to enjoy during the traditional Ho'omaka Foot Ritual.

The aromatic foot scrub and cooling eye mask made her feel like she was in heaven. The massage that followed included warm stones and a mud leg wrap and made her feel like a queen.

By the time she was escorted to her room, she was famished and utterly relaxed. But Jun had thought of that as well, she noted, as room service finished setting up lunch out on the balcony.

She took in the room with its pale yellow walls and cream-colored furnishings. The four-poster bed was a rich dark wood that almost looked black. At the foot of the bed sat a cozy loveseat. Two small double doors swung open from the bathroom and Jun stepped out, offering her a devastating smile as he crossed to her.

"How was it?" He asked, pulling her into his arms for a brief kiss.

"There are no words. It was incredible," she kissed him again. "You didn't have to do that, but I appreciate it."

He smiled and led her to the balcony. "It's my pleasure. I want you to relax and enjoy this week."

With the ocean for company, they dined on fresh seafood while Jun told her what he had planned.

"A four hour hike?"

Jun chuckled. "I promise you'll enjoy it and once you get to the top, you'll be glad I talked you into it. The Kuliouou Trail is a popular destination for a reason."

"Right. No wonder you started with the massage."

He grabbed her hand. "Trust me."

"I do. I also feel like you should redeem one of those sexual favors."

He pulled her up and into the bedroom, then into his arms. He rubbed the tip of his nose against her neck and inhaled.

"I was hoping you'd say that. Knowing you were naked without me for two hours was driving me crazy."

"Tell me what you want," she said, wrapping her arms around his neck.

"You. Just you," he confessed, pulling back to tug the dress up and over her head. He groaned when he found her completely naked underneath it. "Have you been like this the entire day?"

Valerie chuckled and pushed his shorts over his hips. "Maybe."

Jun stepped out of his shorts and pulled his shirt over his head, his expression hot. "Val. Seriously."

"What would you have done if I had been?" She shoved him with both hands so that he fell back on the bed.

Images of his hand up her dress while she rested against him, the flight attendants unknowingly witnessing him touching her, and hot, fast sex in a cramped bathroom filled his vision.

"I assure you everything you're imagining is quite impossible," she said dryly, a smirk on her face.

"I would have found a bathroom at the airport in Sacramento and here in Hawaii and fucked you in there."

His gaze raced over her body, making her hot. "We may have to revisit that little fantasy. I have something else in mind right now. Lay down. Center of the bed."

When he complied, she straddled him, sitting on his chest with her back to him. His breath caught as she wrapped her hand around him and stroked lightly and firmly. She varied the pressure and speed, enjoying the way he moaned her name and how his legs clenched tight with pleasure.

Then she leaned down and braced herself on her left arm. With a light grip on his cock, she flicked her tongue over the tip, tasting and teasing him.

Jun responded immediately by gripping her hips and lifting his head to lap at her, his mind shifting from receiving to giving pleasure and back again. Her moans vibrated around his dick when she took him all the way in her mouth, the warm, wet heat of it making his hips jerk involuntarily.

Mad with desire, he wrapped one of his arms around her waist, pinning her down to him as he devoured her. He thrust his hips slowly, fucking her mouth. The pleasure of this moment was everything, and somehow, he knew it would never be enough.

Valerie balanced as best as she could, relaxed her throat as best as she could, wanting to ride out the insane pleasure as long as possible. She loved it when he lost control like this, loved that she could bring out the animal in him.

The knowledge of that power thrilled her, filled her with a sense of feminine power that threatened to consume her. Desperate to test it out, she placed her hands on his hips to stop his movements.

He stopped and let her go as she shifted positions. She turned around so she could face him and straddled him again. She rocked her hips and his cock slipped over her, making his eyes cross. Desperate to be inside her, he gripped her hips to hold her steady before he came all over them both.

"Valerie," he panted, his voice filled with need. "Let me—I haven't unpacked the condoms. Can you just—" Jun sucked in a breath when her hips moved again, rubbing her pussy over him. "Fuck, Val. Wait a minute."

"No," she said, her eyes burning bright with the knowledge of her power as they met his. "Now."

And then she took him in. Destroyed him as she rode him into oblivion. She was tight and hot and wet. He watched her breast bounce with every movement and while he wanted to touch her, he couldn't stop his nails from digging into her hips as he held onto her like a lifeline.

When she tossed her head back and let loose a triumphant moan as the orgasm ripped through her, his breath lodged in his throat. When she looked down at him, a smug and satisfied smile on her lips, his heart stopped.

Holy fuck, he thought.

She placed her hands on his chest for balance and began riding him again. Jun pulled her down to him and buried his face against her neck while he pistoned his hips, breathing in the scent of her while the fear of his revelation burned in his throat. Then the orgasm hit, and he emptied himself into her.

Terrified that his face might show what he was feeling, Jun held her against him when she would have moved. She snuggled into him, obviously content, and the terror ramped up as the words he knew he shouldn't say clawed their way up his throat, trying to get out.

Fuck. If he stayed here, he wouldn't be able to hold back much longer. He swallowed the words back and took a deep breath, forcing himself to school his features and be calm as he gently nudged her. The minute she rolled off him, he got up to pull on his clothes.

"Why don't you go shower? I'm going to…" he trailed off as he watched her stretch. It made him want to beg for her to—Nope. Don't even think it, he scolded himself. He swallowed again, looking around for his phone. "There's some things I need to check on downstairs."

Valerie pouted. "Why don't you join me?"

He could feel the blush creeping up across his face as the words started choking him. He snatched up his phone and made his way to the door.

"I'll make it up to you, I promise."

Then he was out the door. Jun was dialing Tony before he was even halfway down the hall. He jogged down the stairs while the ringing echoed in his head, cursed when it went to voicemail.

Shaking, he called Dustin instead, accidently hitting video chat. He didn't care. Dustin's face appeared on screen just as he stepped outside.

"Hey, Jun! Wasn't expecting to hear from you. How's—"

"I'm in love with Valerie," he blurted out and sucked in a deep breath, able to breathe now that he had said it out loud. He collapsed in the first shady spot he could find and looked at his friend's shocked expression.

"I can't be in love with Valerie. It's entirely too fast. Who the hell falls in love that fast? It's not healthy or sane. It doesn't make any sense. I've only known her for what… six months? We've been dating a little more than half that time." Jun laughed at himself, relief flooding through him as he made sense of what he was feeling. "Yeah, there's no way this is love."

Dustin started to speak, but Jun continued.

"I mean, I don't even know enough about her to love her. We have things in common, yeah. We wouldn't be dating if we didn't. And we have some similar hobbies and interests. And the chemistry between us is off the charts. I haven't enjoyed sex this much since…well, ever. But there's more to it than that. I mean, what about the other things?"

"What other things?" Dustin asked.

"You know. Politics. Religion. You know, the big things. What if she's a Republican?"

Dustin laughed. "A black Republican?"

Jun scowled. "There are black Republicans."

"Sure. They're out there, but they are a rare breed in California."

"Whatever. You know what I mean."

"Yeah, I do," Dustin agreed, suspecting that his friend was hinting at marriage and children. "But the way I see it, those things don't really matter right now. Even if being in love with her doesn't make sense, you still have time to learn about all of those things."

"It doesn't. I'm not," he insisted.

"Right," Dustin responded, not wanting to push too hard. "But if you were, it doesn't mean you automatically have to move to the next step. You guys will figure out those big things in time, so don't stress about it. Just live in the moment and enjoy your vacation."

Jun scrubbed his hand over his face and caught the scent of her. He licked his lips and tasted her. He glanced at his own image in the video feed and saw that his hair was still a mess from their lovemaking.

He remembered the way she had looked above him, her eyes filled with pride and power as though she had known she had just snatched his heart from his chest. Need, fierce and powerful, rolled in his belly before traveling up to settle in his heart and mind.

None of it mattered, he realized. No matter what he learned about her from this day on, it wouldn't change how he felt about her.

"Ah, fuck," he whispered, closing his eyes in acceptance. "This is real, isn't it? I'm really in love with her."

Dustin merely grinned and hung up.

∞∞∞∞∞∞∞∞

Valerie took her time in the shower, wanting to give Jun the space he so obviously wanted. Feeling foolish, she pulled on the hotel robe and stared at her reflection in the mirror.

She had been so caught up in the moment, so filled with power, that she hadn't considered the consequences of crossing a very intimate and delicate line.

He wanted to get a condom, and she had completely ignored him. Given the awkward way he had left, she assumed he regretted letting her take advantage of him.

Taking a deep breath, she opened the bathroom doors and prepared to face the music. Only the room was still empty. Her suitcase lay open across the bed, while his was still by the wardrobe.

Frowning, she started unpacking her clothes, a nervous ball settling in the pit of her stomach. He should have been back by now. She didn't buy his story about taking care of things. He had two hours during her spa treatment to take care of things.

She couldn't imagine him handling business at the front desk with sex on his breath, so she knew she must have really freaked him out.

Even as she thought it, the door opened. She turned, dress and hanger in her hands, to watch him slip the room key back in his wallet. Their eyes met after he looked up, and she saw something in his demeanor that she couldn't name. He was looking at her differently, and it unnerved her.

"I'm sorry," she blurted out.

Jun stopped and blinked. "For?"

She turned her back to him and put the dress on her hanger. "I crossed a line. You wanted a condom and I didn't listen. But you should know, I'm clean and I'm on the pill. So—"

"Valerie—"

"So there's nothing to worry about. It won't happen again."

He crossed the room and turned her toward him. "I think I've told you before that it pisses me off when you apologize when you don't need to."

Valerie moved back to her suitcase. "You were obviously upset about it."

Jun cringed, embarrassed that he hadn't hid his panic as well as he thought. He hated to lie to her, but he couldn't tell her why he had left. He was certain that she wasn't ready to hear that he had fallen for her. The fact that she was jumping to all the wrong conclusions about how he felt about sex without a condom proved she wasn't ready to hear it.

"I thought you might be upset that I didn't pull out," he lied, hoping she would believe the lame excuse. "I trust you, Valerie. I would have tried to stop you if I didn't. I don't know if I would have stopped—you were sexy as fuck—but I would have tried. Maybe. Probably. And I…I'm glad you trust me. I'm clean, too. I got checked before I left for Crete."

She turned to stare at him as if she could see through the lie. "So we're good?"

"No, not really," he half confessed, crossing the room to her. He untied her robe and moved his hands up her naked flesh, his heart racing. He needed her again. Wanted to love her knowing he was in love with her.

"You opened Pandora's box. If we're going to leave this room at all this week, we'll have to figure out how to close it."

Valerie wrapped her arms around his neck, a coy smile settling on her lips. "I have some ideas."

∞∞∞∞∞∞∞∞

She wouldn't say that they closed it. The sex, which had always been incredible, was somehow elevated to a whole new level. There was an intensity and passion in Jun, freed from the confines of that box that surprised and overwhelmed her.

Maybe it was the long days that kept them in each other's space, but offered no privacy to release the sexual tension that built between them until they returned to their hotel room. Maybe it was just the increased intimacy.

Whatever it was, Valerie knew that there was something different between them. Her instincts told her it wasn't a bad thing, but she just couldn't shake the feeling that she was missing something.

Jun didn't give her many opportunities to dwell on it. She spent the following Sunday morning taking a snorkeling lesson that he had insisted she needed for a snorkel tour later that week.

After lunch, they traveled to Byodo-In Temple. The crowds they found there couldn't compete with the Temple's beauty. Nestled beneath a mountain and surrounded by lush greenery, the bright red building stood out like a beacon of peace and tranquility.

While they waited patiently for their turn to ring the sacred bell, Jun explained to her it's meaning. She hadn't needed him to explain to her that its purpose was to clear the mind of negativity and bring peace.

She felt it each time the sound resonated, but she did enjoy getting to know more about his Japanese heritage.

He took her to Lanikai Beach next. They swam in warm, clear water and relaxed on the beach until sunset. As she cuddled up to him and watched the sun set, she began to understand why he loved beaches.

The water, which had sparkled in varying tones of blue by day, dimmed to almost black as the sun broke over the horizon. It was as if it was willing to be the perfect backdrop for the oranges, reds, and yellows that nearly blinded her with its brilliance.

She thought she would always think of this quiet moment whenever she saw the sun set in the future.

Then there was the hike up Kuliouou Trail, which she had initially dreaded when he had told her that he was taking her there. She had never equated hiking and vacation, but she had enjoyed it more than she would have thought.

She had often lost track of Jun, who, she discovered, was prone to wandering off or trailing behind as he snapped photos. She liked how he got caught up in the beauty that surrounded them, and looked forward to seeing his photos.

When they reached the top of the trail, she simply gawked, never imagining that they would end up peering down at the cities below. It was a view she thought she would only be able to see in photographs.

They had an opulent four-course dinner while they listened to the waves break against the shore at a popular restaurant, and then went to a club in the city where they slow danced to sensual jazz music.

They made the short journey to Manoa Falls one day, and Diamond Head another. He joined her for a second round of snorkeling lessons one morning before taking her to the Pearl Harbor National Memorial.

It wasn't until after the turtle snorkel cruise and the luau that she began to remember that these things cost money, and she had yet to spend a dime on anything more than souvenirs or snacks.

She never saw Jun pay for these excursions up front, so she wasn't sure if he had prepaid or if they were going to be billed to their room. She realized now that when they had planned this trip, they had only talked about airfare and hotel costs. He had never mentioned the car rental or any of the things they had done.

Now, at the end of their trip, Valerie felt unreasonably irritated by the entire thing. She knew— or at least she thought she did—that he didn't mean anything by it. This type of vacation, and all of the money spent, was likely typical for him.

He wasn't used to splitting the costs any more than he was used to being on vacation with someone else. And yet, it still irked her that he hadn't attempted to share those costs with her.

And when she finally got a look at the bill, she nearly exploded with rage.

"What the hell! Do you realize how much money we've spent?"

"Huh?" Jun peaked his head out of the bathroom, toothbrush dangling from his mouth and a towel wrapped around his waist and neck. "What is that?"

"The bill," she explained, scanning over the charges. "Oh, god."

He scowled and snatched it from her hands. "How did you get this?"

"I asked for it." She snatched it back.

"Why?" He made a grab for it, but she moved out of his range. "Val. Let me see it."

"No." Scanning again, she stood by the patio door. "I thought we agreed we weren't doing an all-inclusive."

Jun sighed and went back to the bathroom to spit out the toothpaste. "We agreed that it was too much for you. I decided to cover the remainder of the cost."

Valerie stared at him. "Why?"

"Why not?" He demanded, annoyed. He tied his hair in a tight bun before throwing off the towels to get dressed.

"Because I can't afford it!" She exploded. "You know that. I told you what my budget was for this trip. Why did you add on all of these things without consulting me? I didn't need a $200 massage."

"So? I wanted you to have one, so I paid for it." He tried to take the bill again, but she darted away again. "Damn it, Val. Just let me see it."

She folded it up and stuffed it in her purse. "They're going to email you a copy. I'm keeping this one so I can see how much I owe you."

"For god sakes, you don't owe me anything."

She rounded on him. "The room alone was three thousand. Then you tacked on fifteen hundred dollars worth of excursions, all booked through the resort so I wouldn't know how much it cost."

"Fuck me, Valerie. You're acting like I tricked you or something. I just wanted you to have a good time."

"Oh, yeah, great. Thanks." She slammed her suitcase together and zipped it shut. "Now I have to put off saving for my house because you thought it would be cute to buy me."

His blood went cold. "What the hell did you say?"

"You heard me," she said, pulling her suitcase off the bed. "I didn't need all that shit to have a good time. You did, and I won't be indebted to you because you wanted to throw your money around."

"Are you fucking serious right now?"

Valerie stood by the door with her suitcase and stared at him. "What do you think?"

"I think there's something seriously wrong with you."

Now her eyes turned hard. "I won't be controlled again, Jun. Not with sex, and certainly not with money."

His eyes went flat and he flinched as though she had struck him. Was it the light, or did he look just a little bit pale? She was looking harder when he strode to the bathroom.

They didn't speak as he packed his toiletries and suitcase. They didn't speak as they stood in the elevator on their way to the concierge. Or to the airport. Or on the entire six-hour flight back home.

The strain left her exhausted as they waited for the luggage. He hesitated for the briefest of moments before retrieving her bag from the carousel and passing it to her.

She wondered why that small, hesitant moment felt like he had just slapped her.

She wanted to say something, but couldn't find the words. She wanted him to say something, but he remained stoic and quiet. She started following him to the rideshare pick up location, and stopped short when she heard a car honking behind them and her nephews excitedly shouting her name. She turned toward the car, and then she looked back toward Jun

He kept walking away.

CHAPTER 14

"Oh, honey. You don't really think that he was trying to control you."

Valerie glanced at Gianna and sighed, not surprised that her friend didn't understand. She pulled another shirt out of her hamper, not sure if she should be grateful or annoyed that Maya had called her friends over this morning.

After picking her up from the airport—a request made by Jun before their flight left Hawaii, she learned later—Maya had given her space instead of asking her a million questions.

But there was always a catch with Maya. In this case, it was being ambushed yet again by her and her closest friends the very next day after a restless night of holding back tears that she didn't understand.

"I think that is how it starts," she explained, hanging up her shirt. "Moments like that are small and infrequent at first, and then it just ramps up from there each time you excuse it."

Maya huffed loudly. "Are you seriously comparing him to Damien?"

"They are different people, I know that. But what Jun did was just too similar to Damien for me to excuse."

"Oh, come on, Val," Maya complained.

London spoke up then. "I can see where Val is coming from. He deliberately kept her in the dark because she'd already said no to costly things."

"He just wanted her to have a stress-free vacation," Gianna insisted.

"I would have had a stress-free vacation without half of the expensive excursions. Look, I know it doesn't make sense to you, but I'm telling you this is how it starts. Damien would text me when I was out with friends and I thought it was just the cutest thing. Until it wasn't. I stopped going out because he would call and text me incessantly until I got home. It would be worse with money. I have to draw the line now so that one day he doesn't get to say 'Well, I paid for you to do this, that or the other. Why can't you just blah blah blah.' Whatever. I don't want that."

"You don't really think Jun is like that, do you?" Gianna asked.

Valerie shrugged. "Financially, we'll never be equals. Without appropriate boundaries, we're just asking for problems later down the road, whether intended or not."

"But that's not how you laid it out for him," Maya pointed out, glaring at her. "Jun has been nothing but generous with my boys, with this family. With you. And yet you told him, to his face, that he is no better than your ex. I get you want to protect yourself and set boundaries, Val, but there's a way to do it without punishing him for what some other man did to you."

"That's not—"

"That is exactly what you're doing. It's what you've been doing since you met him. If I'm pissed off by it, I can't imagine how he feels."

She stared at Maya, recalling how Jun looked yesterday, how withdrawn he had been. Sitting next to him, she had felt miles away, and the distance between them grew wider with each passing minute.

Determined to protect her own heart, she had trampled all over his and hurt him. She knew it. And yet she didn't know what else to do. She was so terrified of repeating her past mistakes that she just couldn't stop.

"Oh, honey," London said softly, pulling Valerie down to sit on the bed beside her and pressing the tissue into her hand.

"What?" Valerie looked down at her hand. Stared at the drop of water that landed there. Was she crying?

Strong arms wrapped around her as she started to sob. The dam she had built up around her heart cracked and the tears she hadn't even shed when she had broken up with Damien and left San Diego pushed through until the entire thing came tumbling down.

For the first time in a year, she cried. Cried until her head pounded and heart throat ached from the wailing. When she was empty, she told them everything she hadn't about why and how she had left San Diego. Told them everything he had done since she had left.

Gianna pressed a glass of water and pain meds into her hands. "Drink slowly. You need to get rid of that headache."

Eyes swollen, Valerie sipped gingerly and glanced over at Maya. "Please don't tell, Ruben. The whole thing is embarrassing enough."

"You have absolutely nothing to be embarrassed

about. You were brave and you were smart. You did everything right. I won't say anything. But I think you should tell Jun," she added, squeezing Valerie's knee.

"I know, but not today. I just can't handle any more right now," she confessed, her voice hitching as fresh tears filled her eyes.

"Of course, honey. You lay down," Gianna insisted, pulling back the covers. "We'll put your laundry away and get you a snack. Then you go to bed. You can talk to him another day. Right now, let's take care of you."

Valerie nodded and laid her head on the pillow with a deep sigh. She closed her eyes, holding back the tears. The exhaustion and strain of the last two days settled on her like a weight and she was asleep within minutes.

∞∞∞∞∞∞∞

Jun moved through the week on autopilot, and avoided the Halls at all costs. Knowing no other way to cope with the emotions that warred inside him, he made excuses to work long hours at the office and had gone out to dinner every night that week.

He realized by Wednesday that the isolation only made things worse, but couldn't seem to shake himself out of self-pity. His emotions ran the gamut from hurt to anger, from love to despair, and absolutely everything in between.

It wasn't fair that he should spend one week gallivanting around and romancing the woman he loved in Hawaii, and then spend the next feeling like the same woman had carved out his heart with a spoon.

He tried, and failed, not to think about it, or her. But when he had finally gotten around to doing his laundry Saturday morning, he discovered that the scent of her lingered on his clothing.

He was reminded of where they had been or what they had been doing when he had been wearing the things he tossed into the washing machine. He hoped to god that the detergent washed her scent away. He prayed to god that it wouldn't.

And then there were the photos. On his camera and his phone. He had captured her unaware several times during the trip. He had photos of her lounging on the beach or pausing on their hikes to gaze at nature. He had captured a few of her reading inscriptions, her face a picture of concentration.

He had even managed to get a few with the two of them together. How had she not seen the love that he now saw shining in his eyes? It had been such a long time since he had been in love, and that only made it harder for him to keep his feelings to himself.

But he had wanted her to be happy and enjoy their time together more than he had wanted to confess how he felt. So he had taken Dustin's advice and lived in the moment, and tried to show her how much he loved her instead.

He failed at that too, all thanks to the fact that she couldn't or wouldn't believe that he wasn't her ex.

Thinking about it always enraged him. He loved her, and suspected he might be willing to do just about anything to keep her, but he drew the line at paying for her ex's crimes.

There was no point in trying to build anything with her if she was just going to be waiting for him to do whatever it was her ex had done to her.

He let himself wallow in anger and self-pity and defeat with the understanding that he would be done with it by the end of the week.

His doorbell rang, and Jun knew before he checked that it would be Maya. She had come by every day this week and he had watch her from the app on his phone, both grateful and annoyed.

She waited about five minutes before shooting him a text, telling him that she just wanted to check on him. But she wasn't the woman he wanted coming to his door. She wasn't the woman he wanted to check up on him.

But he was home this time, and since today was the last day he was allowed to wallow, he opened the door.

"Well, you don't look like complete shit," she said, looking him up and down.

Jun appreciated the first real smile he had in a week. "Gee, thanks."

"Oh, I wouldn't thank me yet," she said with a grin, stepping into the house and forcing him to step back.

He sensed her before she appeared at the door. Every muscle in his body tightened, hardened in self-defense when Valerie and Maya switched places.

He simply stared at her as she cast a tentative glance his way before turning to shut the door after Maya left. The soft click jump-started his heart, sent it racing painfully inside his chest. He needed her to stay. He wanted her to leave.

She couldn't look at him, not yet, so Valerie leaned back against his door and looked at his feet.

"I need to say some things. A lot of things. Will you hear me out?" When he didn't move or respond, she continued. "First off, I'm sorry for ever comparing you to my ex, and for overreacting to the whole money thing. I just panicked, and wasn't thinking clearly, and just immediately jumped to all of the wrong conclusions because I didn't want to make the same mistake again. I realized this week that I haven't let go or moved on like I thought, and you deserve to know why because until I do, I will probably keep fucking this up. Can we…Can I sit down?"

Jun noticed then that she was visibly shaking and her eyes looked swollen. Watching her closely, he moved to the living room and sat on the edge of the couch. She joined him, but kept her gaze trained on the floor in front of her feet.

"I met Damien at a bar in Little Italy. He looks like a dark chocolate version of Shemar Moore, and oozed so much effortless charm that women basically lined up to talk to him. When I finally got my turn…I completely fell for the act. God, he was smooth, and when he worked in sex? It was easy to believe him when he said he wanted and needed me all to himself.

"When he would text or call me when I was out with friends, at first I just thought he missed me. See, Damien is a Sailor in the Navy, and his underway schedule kept him out at sea for weeks, sometimes months, so I believed him when he said our time together was so valuable to him or that he was worried I'd find and leave him for someone else. But no matter how I tried to reassure him, he never let up. He started calling or texting me nonstop until I got home. Or he would show up where I was and beg to take me home so we could have sex. He started asking for pictures so he could see who I was with or whether I was really at home like I said I was. It stressed me out so much that I just stopped going out."

She paused and took a deep, shaky breath. Jun knew from the vacant look on her face that she had gone back to that moment, reliving it. He wanted to shake her until she came back. Wanted to erase every moment so she would never go back there again.

"And it just got worse. He'd complain about what I'd wear because he thought I was trying to seduce other men. Accused me of cheating on him if I missed his phone call. Every argument ended with sex and so of course I believed every little whisper of love and devotion. Believed that the man who touched me so intimately, who paid such attention to my pleasure, really did love me.

"But deep down I knew better. The little voice that screamed 'Get out!' just got louder and louder until I couldn't take it anymore.

"I avoided him for as long as I could, putting off the inevitable. He showed up one day and I told him I wanted to break up. He became this entirely different person. Or maybe he finally showed me who he really was. He forced his way into the apartment, shoved me back when I tried to stop him from coming in. We were so busy yelling and screaming at each other that I didn't realize that he was backing me up toward my bedroom until I heard Claudia yelling.

"She told him to get out, but he ignored her and grabbed my arm, tried to force me into my room. When I tried to get my arm free, he...he slapped me."

Valerie touched her face. Felt the sting as if it had just happened.

"I...I'm not sure what happened next, exactly. I

was so lost in the pain and shock and humiliation. I just saw his lips moving before he threw me on the ground. Then he was gone, and Claudia was sitting next to me. She was on the phone with the police."

When Valerie lay back against the couch and pressed the heels of her hands to her eyes, Jun had to stop himself from scooping her up into his arms. He wanted to touch her, but didn't think he should. How had she ever let him touch her after being a victim of domestic violence?

If Claudia hadn't been there, Damien would have raped her. It wouldn't have been like the other times when their arguments had ended in sex.

"Can I get you some water?" He asked, wanting to give her a break. Wanting to give himself something to do.

She nodded, staring blankly at the ceiling. As he filled a glass, he wondered how much more there was to this story. Careful not to touch her, he sat beside her and offered the water. She only glanced at him briefly before taking the cup and a small sip.

"I spent the next six months erasing any connection to him or anything that he knew about me. Phone numbers, email addresses, bank accounts, physical address, and social media. He tried to reach out to me through all of it. He showed up at my job one time. When he came by the apartment again, I told him that if he didn't stop, I was going to get a restraining order. His eyes had been so cold. So full of hate. He said he would give me time to come to my senses. I realized then that I had to go, or it would never, really end, so I moved here and thought that was the end of it."

"Oh, god, Valerie." How could there be more?

Hadn't the man done enough to ruin her life?

But there was more. She told him about the emails from her former roommate, the break in at her job, and the tile tracker disguised in the letter from her alumni association.

The rage filled him, making him nauseous with its toxicity. He wished he had a face for the body he was picturing himself pummeling into the ground. How could she sit there so calmly when Damien was hunting for her?

"Claudia emailed me this morning. When she came home from the gym, Damien was leaving the apartment. Apparently he had his friend sleep with the new roommate last night so he could let Damien into the apartment this morning. He broke into her room, rifled around her desk, and tried to get on her computer. Luckily, she keeps it passcoded, so he couldn't get in. She's pretty freaked out and insisting I go down there to file the restraining order."

"She's right. When are you going? Do you need me to go with you?"

Valerie looked at him finally and the dam broke again. She saw the moment of shocked panic on his face before he took the glass from her and pulled her into his lap. She sobbed into his shoulder, soaking his shirt while he gently stroked her back.

"I'm sorry," she said, pushing away and off the couch. "I'm a mess. This is a mess. I didn't mean to blubber all over you. I just thought you should know. I wanted you to understand why this just won't work out."

"Is that what you want?" He asked quietly.

Valerie looked at him, really looked at him. He sat on the couch with one foot tucked under his leg in faded black sweatpants. His white t-shirt was plastered to his shoulder thanks to her tears. His hair was tied in a ponytail at the nape of his neck. He watched her, his eyes just a little bit sad. She knew then that she wanted more than she dared ask for.

"Isn't that what you want? I'm a mess, Jun. I can't promise or guarantee that I won't slip and do or say something stupid because of what I went through with Damien. How could you want to put up with that?"

Jun rose and crossed to her. "How could you let me touch you? That man…what he did to you? How could you ever trust any man ever again?"

"It…" She trailed off, trying to find the words. "I don't know. It's different with you. I've always felt safe."

He placed his hands on her shoulders and drew her to him, resting his forehead against hers. "It's different with you, too."

"I don't want to hurt you again."

"Then tell me that this is what you want." *Tell me you love me,* he thought.

"It is. But—"

Jun brushed his lips across hers to silence her. "No buts."

Valerie wrapped her arms around his neck and pressed herself against him, deepening the kiss. She needed him to touch her, to fill all the cold places inside her so she would feel warm again. Desperate for his heat, she let go of him to tug at his shirt.

But instead of lifting his arms, he took her hand and led her upstairs. The moment they crossed the threshold, she dived at him, urging him toward the bed as she kissed him.

He responded with slow, lazy kisses, pulling her on top of him when he sat on the bed. His hands slipped under her shirt and he touched her softly, lightly, his fingers like a delicate feather as they moved up her spine.

Anxious for more, she lifted her arms so he could pull her shirt over her head. She again tried to push him down on the bed, but he was like a mountain and wouldn't be budged.

Jun placed his hands on either side of her face and pulled her down for a kiss. Slow again, needing to take his time with her, wanting to cherish her. He trailed soft kisses across her cheek and down her neck and then back again until he felt her melt into him. The pace set, he turned and laid her out on his bed.

With soft, soft kisses and slow patient caresses, he worshiped her body, filled all those dark, cold places inside her with heat. Heart racing, body flushed with pleasure, she cried out his name. Begged him for more. When he finally filled her, she thought she might weep from joy. When they came together, she nearly did.

Curled up against his side, it didn't take Valerie long to drift off to sleep. Jun imagined that the strain and stress had more to do with her exhaustion than their lovemaking. He slipped from bed, dressed quickly and jogged downstairs to retrieve his phone. He shot Maya a quick text that he was heading over to grab some things for Valerie before he left the house.

Maya was waiting for him at the door. The look she sent him told him she suspected he was up to something.

"Where's Val?"

"Sleeping. I just came over to get her PJs," he added, stepping inside.

"I'll get them."

"No, it's okay," he insisted. "She told me where they are."

"Do you want to tell me why my baby sister has cried her eyes out twice this week?" Ruben demanded as he came down the hall. He leveled a glare at Jun when they turned to look at him. "Maya insists you're not the cause, which is why I haven't sliced your tires. Or your throat. What's going on?"

Jun's eyes went hard with anger. "Don't worry about it. I'm going to take care of it."

Ruben grinded his teeth together in annoyance. "Maya had that same murderous look on Sunday. If anybody is going to kill someone on my sister's behalf, it's going to be me."

"I'll explain later," she said, pleased with what she saw on Jun's face, and held out a flash drive to him. "Pretty sure this is everything you'll need."

Jun blinked at her. "What?"

"I got the truth out of her on Sunday, and I've spent the week looking for a name and address. You're going to want to get to him before I do."

"Get to who? What is that?"

"But how?" Jun, asked, ignoring him.

Maya shrugged, the casual movement belying the vicious glint in her eyes. "She may have left her computer open when I insisted she go talk to you, so I did some digging."

"Oh, Maya, I absolutely love you." He took the flash drive. "You are amazing."

"I know."

CHAPTER 15

She had kept everything, and had documented or gathered even more evidence. Jun read through every vicious email, every social-media dig and wondered what it might be like to kill a man.

She had gone back and pulled her phone records as far back as she could to document the numerous times he texted or called her. There were scanned copies of her contracts with the P.O. box, bank, and cell phone carrier—everything she had changed to prevent him from being able to contact or find her.

Each time he looked at her or held her in his arms, he marveled at her courage and strength. He understood why they called women in her situation survivors. She refused to be a victim of domestic violence, and he admired everything she had done to keep it from making her one.

It made him want to slay the dragon. He knew she would be pissed when she learned what he and Maya and Claudia had done. When she learned what he had yet to do.

But because he was desperate for her to love him in return, he needed to ensure that her ex would never be able to come between them. Once she closed this chapter of her life, she would be free to love him.

At least he hoped she would be.

She was more open with him now that he knew the truth. They talked about Hawaii, and he assured her his intent had only been to give her the best possible vacation experience. He admitted that he had gone overboard on the price, and while he couldn't promise that he wouldn't be tempted to do it again, he would try to make his plans more transparent in the future.

She hadn't been thrilled with the compromise and had only agreed to it because he agreed to let her pay him back for some of the costs they had racked up in Hawaii. He could tell that she was a little bit disappointed about dipping into her down payment savings, but since he saw her moving in with him in the future, he knew she wouldn't have to worry.

Over the course of the last two weeks, he reached out to everyone he had known in high school and in college, searching for some sort of six degrees of separation miracle. The evidence that Valerie had was overwhelming, but he didn't trust the military or police force brotherhood to do the right thing.

Isn't that why so many women refused to come forward about crimes against them? He never truly understood or appreciated their struggle until now. He just wanted to give her a fair shot at justice.

Jun checked his phone as they waited to disembark from the plane in San Diego, grinned when the final piece of his plan fell into place.

"What are you smiling about?" Valerie asked.

He kissed her nose. "Just realized I get to see you

half naked on a San Diego beach after all."

Valerie wrinkled her nose, and then stared blankly ahead. "This isn't a vacation."

Jun rubbed her back. "I know. Don't worry, Val. You'll get through this."

She took a deep breath, grateful for his presence, for the reassuring warmth of his hand. Coming back to San Diego was harder than it had been to leave. She had lived with the hope that she wouldn't have to take legal action against Damien, and could have, she realized, easily lived her life without ever having done so.

But Jun had changed everything. He had come into her life and made her feel things, such strong things, that didn't make any sense to her. His honest and raw attraction to her, and the confusion and hesitation he felt around it, had softened her heart since the beginning.

And every day since, he showed her what real, selfless love should look like. So of course she had fallen in love with him.

Valerie had realized it when he asked if he could go with her to San Diego. There had been no judgment, no hesitation. Just an offer of a helping hand. And in that moment, she had felt completely invincible. Filled with the love of him, she knew she could and would do anything to keep him.

And that meant facing her demons. She wasn't afraid of Damien anymore. He held no power over her anymore. But she was afraid that she was entering a long, uphill battle to get him out of her life.

He wasn't going to go quietly. She didn't look forward to court dates, even with Jun by her side. She just wanted it done and over with so she could start a life with him.

Weary from a fight that hadn't even begun, she remained quiet and stoic on the drive, blankly watching the city go by. It wasn't until Jun parked that she realized they were at Liberty Station. She sat up, blinking at him as he climbed from the car and came around to open her door.

"What are we doing here?" She asked as she got out of the car.

"I'm told this is a great place for eats. But first, coffee," he added, taking her hand and pulling her with him. "I didn't get a lot of sleep last night."

Valerie grinned, knowing she had been the cause of his sleepless night. "You are absolutely welcome."

He grinned in response and ushered her toward a table. "You want your usual?"

"Yeah, sounds good."

Jun stood in line and pulled out his phone. His eyes lit up in alarm when he saw he had several missed calls from Claudia. They had been contacting each other in secret since he got access to Valerie's files, working together to execute his plans. They both accepted that the promise of incurring Valerie's wrath paled in comparison to the benefits they hoped to reap from the end result. But they rarely called or text each other, sticking to email instead in order to have the paper trail. Knowing it must be important, he opened up his messages.

Claudia: HE KNOWS! DON'T GO! HE KNOWS SHE'S HERE!

Oh, fuck!

Jun whipped around as the entrance door swung open. Damien towered in the doorway, his rage filled eyes scanning the restaurant for Valerie as he moved inside. They saw each other at the same time. She jumped up from her chair as he charged toward her.

"You stupid fucking bitch! What the hell did you do?"

He grabbed her arm, yanking her to him just as Jun stepped up behind her.

Jun placed a hand on Valerie's shoulder and spoke as calmly as possible. "You're going to want to let her go, Damien."

"I don't know who the fuck you are, but you better back the fuck off," he snarled.

"I'm the reason she's here, and the reason your ass is in so much trouble," he said quietly, pleased when Damien's attention focused solely on him. "Let. Her. Go."

Valerie took his moment of distraction to take hold of the arm that had hers for balance and delivered a swift, hard kick to Damien's groin. He let go of her, buckling in pain and grabbing his bruised dick. She shoved him as hard as he could, releasing all the pent up rage and fear. He flipped over a recently vacated chair and crumpled to the ground.

"You bitch!" He groaned in pain.

"That's enough, son."

Heart racing, Valerie turned toward the voice and found a sharply dressed man. His black suit was crisp and clean, and perfectly tailored to his body. Though she didn't know what any of it meant, she knew from the insignia hanging over his heart that he was a high-ranking member of the Navy. With a folder and his hat tucked under his arm, he peered down at Damien. The coffee shop was suddenly abuzz with activity as officers came in and lifted Damien from the ground. He didn't speak or look up as they ushered him out.

The man bent over to right the chair, then turned toward Valerie.

"You must be Valerie. And Jun. Nice to see you again," he added, shaking Jun's hand. "Why don't we have us a seat so we can be done with this little matter."

Valerie blinked at him, then Jun as they sat. "This is Captain Burton Larter. I…uh…contacted him about Damien."

Burton snorted, setting his hat and folder on the table as he sat. "More like tracked me down like a rogue gator. Insisted I come all the way down from Florida to have a little chat with Damien's command."

"What? Why? I…I don't understand what is happening." Valerie turned toward Jun. "What did you do?"

Jun took her hand, hoping she would understand. "I just wanted to make sure that there wouldn't be any problems when you filed the restraining order. Captain Burton was a senior in high school when I met him, and I remembered he'd joined the Navy. So I tracked him down, got his take on what would happen if you filed, and asked him to come here to make sure we did everything right."

"The man wouldn't listen to reason," he said, opening the folder. "Everything you've got is more than enough for the MPO, but he just kept insisting it be handled by someone he trusted. Damien was supposed to be detained early this morning. I can only assume that someone tipped him off. It would seem Jun's concerns were warranted."

"Okay. Um. Wow. What's an MPO?"

"Military Protective Order. It is similar to a civilian

restraining order, but without the hearing process. And after what I witnessed today, I'm requesting his transfer to Florida where he will receive my special brand of counseling."

Burton pushed the folder toward her. She read over it, saw that it had been completed with concise details of her history with Damien that justified the request. It was everything she needed, but without the fight. Well, there had been a fight, she thought, as the adrenaline left her body, leaving her with a low-grade headache.

"So I sign this and that's it?" She asked, unsure.

"Yes ma'am. And I'll take any hard copies of your documentation."

"Oh, right." Jun pulled his messenger bag onto his lap and took out a large folder. He looked over at Valerie. "Okay?"

"How in the—" She cut herself, not wanting to get into it right now. Signing the form, she pushed the folder back to Burton.

"Perfect." Burton gathered everything up and stood. "I have a sister and a daughter. I would never wish for them to go through what you have, but if they do, I hope they have even an ounce of your bravery and wit. Jun, I'll be looking forward to those tickets you promised."

∞∞∞∞∞∞∞

He drove them to their hotel. She didn't speak. Just sat and stared out the window, hands folded calmly in her lap. It was making him crazy. He was prepared for her to kick and scream and yell. And rightfully so. He had deliberately gone behind her back, giving out information that she didn't know that he had access to, and completely changed what she had come here to do.

So why was she just sitting there?

Jun pulled into the hotel parking lot, found a spot easily. She climbed out and headed inside. He retrieved their bags from the trunk and followed after her, hanging back as she checked them in.

In the elevator, she pressed the button, staring at the doors until they opened again. By the time they reached their room, he was literally sweating with panic, sure that she was either going to kill him, or break up with him.

He would much rather she killed him than live without her.

Valerie tossed her purse on the bed and turned to face him. "So if I am understanding everything that just happened correctly, you got into my computer and used that information to make arrangements with your high school friend because you didn't think I had enough for a civilian restraining order."

Jun pushed their bags into a corner and prepared to face the music.

"Close. Maya got into your computer. I had every confidence that you had everything you needed, but I didn't trust the system to do right by you. I have also been talking with Claudia. She left me a voicemail saying that after Damien realized he was in trouble, he went to her place and threatened her. She knew who I was meeting, so she gave him the address, knowing he'd get caught there. I didn't get her warning in time or I wouldn't have taken you there, wouldn't have put you in danger like that had I known."

He stopped to take a deep breath, trying and

failing to stop rambling. "But god, seeing you nail him like that makes it almost worth not hitting him myself. You don't want to know how much I've been dreaming of hurting him. Look, I know I crossed a line, going behind your back and everything like that, but I would absolutely do anything to protect the woman I love. So. Sorry. Not sorry. I had to do it. I needed to do it. So. Yeah."

Valerie crossed her arms and just stared at him. Waited. She could practically see the wheels turning in his head as he looked back at her, wondering why she wasn't speaking.

As the silence stretched on, she imagined that he was recalling what he just said to her. Then she saw the moment he understood. His eyes lit up, a little light bulb in his brain, when he realized what he had confessed.

Jun slid his hands into the pockets of his cotton shorts and rocked on his heels. Though he had imagined telling her that he loved her in ways so much better than this, he wouldn't blush this time.

He meant what he said, and he wasn't taking it back. He wasn't going to hide it anymore. She was just going to have to deal with it. He stared back at her, daring her to acknowledge what he said.

Then she sighed heavily. "How is that you're always one step ahead of me?" She asked, uncrossing her arms. "It's really unfair."

Jun's heart pounded as she closed the distance between them. "Doesn't matter. Just catch up."

"No, that's not good enough." Valerie slipped her arms around his neck. "You've reached every milestone just ahead of me, so there really is only one choice. I have to surpass you. I have to beat you to the next milestone."

Jun blinked, curious to find out where this was heading. "And what exactly is the next milestone?"

"Well, I love you," she said, kissing him softly, and watched him close his eyes, the relief evident on his face. "So obviously I'm going to have to insist that you marry me. We can pick out the ring this afternoon, or wait until we get back to Sacramento, but the end result will be the same. You're my fiancé. Do you think that is going to be a problem for you?"

Jun rested his forehead against hers. Grinned as his heart filled with joy.

"I think that is going to be one wedding I can look forward to."

ABOUT THE AUTHOR

Born and (mostly) raised in Sacramento, California in the 1980s, the world was my oyster. I grew up in a wonderfully culturally diverse neighborhood and as a result, I had a friend from (and a crush on) every ethnic group. And then, thanks to the advent of personal computers and dial up Internet, my world grew even bigger. I spent a lot of time in front of my computer watching anime, chatting on AIM messenger or chat rooms, downloading music from Napster, and writing poetry and fan fiction.

Naturally, this shaped me and kept my mind open and accepting. And love? That was maybe the one thing that was actually colorblind.

But as life would show me over the next several decades, love is a little more nuanced than that. So with my ever-increasing interest in the written language, I wrote about it. And drawn back to Sacramento, one of America's most diverse cities, I felt the need to dedicate a space that celebrated not only love, but this wonderfully diverse place that no one outside of California seems to know is the capital.

I want you to get to know my city, and maybe, you'll fall in love with the 916 too.

DD DAVIS

#SACRAMENTO

SACRAMENTO, CA
visitsacramento.com
Sacramento is the star on the map of California - where you will find cultural attractions to inspire you, cutting-edge cuisine to impress you, history to enrich you and surprises to put a smile on your face. Venture out in any direction and you'll see why we're so fond of saying, "California begins here."

Driving from Sacramento to:
- Napa Valley Wine Country, ~1 hour
- San Francisco, ~1.5 hours
- Lake Tahoe Ski Resorts, ~2 hours
- Yosemite National Park, ~2.5 hours

Flying from Sacramento to:
- Los Angeles, ~1 hour
- Las Vegas, ~ 1.5 hours
- San Diego, ~1.5 hours
- Hawaii, ~5 hours

NATOMAS, SACRAMENTO, CA
visitsacramento.com
Natomas is home to parks and trails, family-friendly eateries and shopping areas, sure to please visitors and locals alike.

If you're hungry, check out its many taquerias and food trucks or head to the La Superior market along Northgate Boulevard to shop for authentic Mexican foods.

If you're the outdoorsy type, Discovery Park, one of the region's largest green spaces, is the perfect place to perch during a hot Sacramento summer day. A part of the American River Parkway, the park offers a variety of recreational activities including boating, picnic areas and wading in the river. It's also home to the emerald and very Instagram-worthy Jibboom Street Bridge.

In the summer, the 47+ acre North Natomas Regional Park hosts some of the community's biggest events, including movie nights and farmers markets. The park also offers its own sports fields, bikeways, play areas, water features, and some of the best play areas for both your kiddos and doggos.

Natomas can be accessed directly off Interstate 5 and off Garden Highway.

NORTH NATOMAS REGIONAL PARK
cityofsacramento.org
This 212.31 acre park has the several amenities such as
softball fields, large and small dog parks with, farmer's market, picnic area, playground, water spray area, and a stage with lawn amphitheater.

NORTH NATOMAS COMMUNITY CENTER AND AQUATICS COMPLEX
bcaarchitects.com

The new North Natomas Community Center and Aquatics Complex will be home to the only Olympic size pool in Sacramento. The new $32 million complex, which will be located adjacent to the 220-acre North Natomas Regional Park, will feature a 10,600 square foot community center, a competition pool, a recreational pool, on-site parking and support facilities. Estimated completion date: 2021.

SACRAMENTO INTERNATIONAL AIRPORT
sacramento.aero/smf
With easy freeway access, convenient parking, and the most flyer-friendly experience, Sacramento International Airport makes every journey as easy as SMF.

GOLDEN 1 CENTER
golden1center.com
Golden 1 Center sits proudly in the heart of downtown Sacramento, less than a mile from California's first thriving business district.

It's here that you'll find people from all walks of life building a community around their favorite things: Music, sports, entertainment, culture, food, and beverage. A homage to the city's legacy and a marvel of its bright future, Golden 1 Center represents everything that makes Sacramento the next Great American City. From design to sustainability to connectivity to cuisine, it's a celebration of what Sacramento does best.

SACRAMENTO KINGS
www.nba.com/kings
The Sacramento Kings are an American professional basketball team.

DOWNTOWN COMMONS
docosacramento.com
It's a night on the town with best friends or a seat in the plaza with coffee and a sketchpad. Seeing your favorite band for the first time. Sitting outside in the warm air with a craft cocktail. Surrounding yourself in amazing art and architecture. Staying at one of the most eclectic hotels in California. Shopping at one-of-a-kind boutiques alongside the most recognized global brands. DOCO is where the locals hang out and visitors from around the globe experience this region at its finest. Sacramento is the next Great American City…and DOCO is our common ground.

CHASING OLIVES PHOTOGRAPHY
chasingolivesphotography.com
We are Chasing Olives Photography, a husband and wife partnership. On-location portrait photography in natural light is our favorite -- but we do so much more! We believe everyone should have beautiful photos, so we provide stunning, high-quality pictures at a very affordable rate. We serve Sacramento and the surrounding areas. We photograph engagements, families, maternity, headshots, seniors, and even pets (just to name a few)! We also photograph small events!

MALT & MASH IRISH PUB

maltmash.com

Malt and Mash is Downtown Sacramento's favorite neighborhood Irish bar. Featuring 150 types of whiskeys from around the world, 15 local and craft beers on tap, and plenty of TV's with all the games. We also feature live bands , DJ's, and huge outdoor festivals in the park.

Located a block away from the Golden 1 Center and situated in the vibrant entertainment district of the 700 block, Malt and Mash is the ideal location to meet up with your friends before any event at Golden 1.

PIZZA ROCK

pizzarocksacramento.com

While Pizza Rock is a restaurant first and foremost, it's about more than just food; it is a destination location where guests come to unwind, have something to eat, drink, and also sit back and enjoy the scene around them. There is an electric energy inside the space, including a tremendous sound system. Guests are encouraged to come for the food and stay for the fun.

DELTA SHORES

deltashoressacramento.com

A master-planned 800-acre mixed-use development that aims to be the premier Power Center in Sacramento featuring best-in-class community & lifestyle retailers, services, entertainment and restaurants. The project is one of the region's largest new retail developments and is located in one of the last large in-fill sites in the City of Sacramento.

PUNCH BOWL SOCIAL

punchbowlsocial.com

Courtside to the Kings Golden 1 Center, Punch Bowl Social Sacramento is all about red carpet treatment for all of the Legends-In-Our-Own-Minds. This 25,000-square-foot hot spot is set up with bowling, billiards, darts, ping-pong, karaoke and other games that'll have you running point all night. And because amazing food and craft cocktails always take things to the next level, we've got those covered too. Score.

THE KAY

downtownsac.org

By day, The Kay buzzes with activity from the mix of mid-rise and high-rise office buildings. After dark, The Kay draws its energy from a diverse mix of hotels, restaurants, nightlife and entertainment venues. The Kay District is eclectic and a study of contrast. Visitors can dine in a sleek modern restaurant with historic landmarks in the background, spend the night in a hotel which once was a public market, or catch a live show in one of Sacramento's historic vaudeville houses. The Kay District encompasses L Street to J Street between 13th and 7th Street.

DIVE BAR

divebarsacramento.com

Dive Bar in downtown Sacramento welcomes guests with modern elegance, and a fantasy twist! Splash into our venue, where we make Mermaid Magic every night in our 40 ft saltwater aquarium. Our live underwater performers will transport you to a sea of dreams with their world-famous shows, while our bartenders mix up their own aquatic alchemy behind the bar. With live DJs, dazzling tank light-shows, monthly and weekly drink specials and events, you can look no further for the best nightlife venue on land...or sea.

FOUNTAINS AT ROSEVILLE

fountainsatroseville.com

Shop, Dine, and Play at Fountains at Roseville, a unique collection of 40 stores & 10 restaurants. With so many choices, this is your premiere destination for shopping and casual and fine dining.

ELK GROVE, CA

exploreelkgrove.com

In the heart of California, Elk Grove is nestled between wine country and the waterways of the California Delta. A tech-savvy city with a small-town feel, Elk Grove is diverse, personable and never too busy for the finer things in life. Explore, uncover and enjoy.